The Green Berets

The Green Berets

◆

Action in Iraq

A look at the chaotic life inside a Special Forces A-team

Jay Mann

iUniverse, Inc.
New York Lincoln Shanghai

The Green Berets
Action in Iraq

Copyright © 2007 by Jay Mann

All rights reserved. No part of this book may be used or reproduced by any means, graphic, electronic, or mechanical, including photocopying, recording, taping or by any information storage retrieval system without the written permission of the publisher except in the case of brief quotations embodied in critical articles and reviews.

iUniverse books may be ordered through booksellers or by contacting:

iUniverse
2021 Pine Lake Road, Suite 100
Lincoln, NE 68512
www.iuniverse.com
1-800-Authors (1-800-288-4677)

Because of the dynamic nature of the Internet, any Web addresses or links contained in this book may have changed since publication and may no longer be valid.

Certain characters in this work are historical figures, and certain events portrayed did take place. However, this is a work of fiction. All of the other characters, names, and events as well as all places, incidents, organizations, and dialogue in this novel are either the products of the author's imagination or are used fictitiously.

ISBN: 978-0-595-44634-6 (pbk)
ISBN: 978-0-595-68994-1 (cloth)
ISBN: 978-0-595-88959-4 (ebk)

Printed in the United States of America

To Bill O'Reilly—a true American, a true patriot, and a best friend to the military.

Acknowledgments

A special thanks to all the Green Berets who have ever worked beside me, led me, followed me, complimented me, criticized me, and generally put up with me. No words are good enough for the men on the A-team.

It is the soldier, not the reporter,
Who has given us freedom of the press.

It is the soldier, not the poet,
Who has given us freedom of speech.

It is the soldier, not the campus organizer,
Who has given us freedom to demonstrate.

It is the soldier, not the lawyer,
Who has given us the right to a fair trial.

It is the soldier who salutes the flag,
Who serves under the flag,
Whose coffin is draped by the flag,
Who allows the protester to burn the flag.

Charles M. Province

Special Forces A-teams (Green Berets) or Operational Detachment Alphas (ODAs) are organized into twelve-man teams that can be deployed throughout the world and can operate independently. They can perform a variety of missions including counter-terrorism, direct action, foreign internal defense, special reconnaissance, and unconventional warfare.

The following is a breakdown of the twelve members that compose an A-team:

Officer: Rank of captain. The one who is, overall, responsible for the team. Leader of the team.

Warrant Officer: The warrant officer acts as the team leader in the absence of the captain. In the event the team is split into two elements, the warrant officer will lead one of these elements.

Operations Sergeant: A senior sergeant first class or master sergeant. The team operations sergeant is responsible for all personnel and day-to-day operations.

Intelligence Sergeant: A staff sergeant or sergeant first class. The intelligence sergeant is responsible for the collection and storage of all classified material and advises the captain on all intelligence-related issues.

Senior and Junior Weapon Sergeants: Sergeant, staff sergeant, or sergeant first class. These two are responsible for the maintenance and accountability of all the team's weapon systems and optics. They advise the captain on tactics and security issues.

Senior and Junior Engineer Sergeants: Sergeant, staff sergeant, or sergeant first class. Engineer sergeants maintain accountability of all the team's equipment and advise the captain on construction and demolition projects.

Senior and Junior Medical Sergeants: Sergeant, staff sergeant, or sergeant first class. The medical sergeants are responsible for the health and welfare of the team. They are experts in medical trauma treatment.

Senior and Junior Communications Sergeants: Sergeant, staff sergeant, or sergeant first class. Communications sergeants are responsible for all of the communications and computer systems.

Team Introduction

Captain Rinehart—team leader

Sergeant First Class John Smith—operations sergeant

Staff Sergeant Jeff Wallace—senior weapons sergeant

Staff Sergeant Miguel Sanchez—junior weapons sergeant

Sergeant First Class Eddie Hardy—senior engineer sergeant

Staff Sergeant Wally Granner—junior engineer sergeant

Sergeant First Class Mike Vomage—senior medical sergeant

Staff Sergeant Larry Masson—junior medical sergeant

Sergeant First Class Shebley Henderson—senior communications sergeant

Staff Sergeant Bruce Stern—junior communications sergeant

PART I
Killing and Clearing

A coward will excuse his actions behind an aggressive person's behavior.

—*Jason Bitterman*

1

Karmah, Iraq: April 2004

The mosque was new, probably built within the last couple of years. It wasn't the most elaborate the soldiers of ODA 451 had seen in Iraq, just a small *masjid*. But it was still nicely set up, and at this moment it was the only mosque that mattered.

A six-foot-high wall surrounded the mosque, and it appeared to have only one gate. Typical of Iraqi mosques, steel crossbeams covered with sheet metal comprised the gate. A wall one hundred meters long by fifty meters wide enclosed the compound's five buildings-the dome and minaret from which calls to pray would issue, plus a bathroom facility, a two-story building that appeared to be a barracks, and two smaller outbuildings. The outbuildings' purpose was unclear. They could have been used for vehicle maintenance, as storage facilities, or they could even house the imam of the mosque.

The soldiers had been receiving sporadic small arms fire for the past two hours from across one hundred fifty meters of flat, featureless field that separated them from the long side of the compound. John, the team sergeant, was getting tired of shooting people who kept appearing in the windows. He would shoot one guy, and a few minutes later another one would show in the same place. He would shoot that one, and more would appear in a seemingly endless stream of opposition.

Last year when he was just a team member, rather than team sergeant, John would have considered this fun. But now that he was in charge, moving the battle forward was his responsibility. John knew this wouldn't last—something would give eventually. If they just kept up this stalemate, they would resolve nothing.

The other four members of the John's team were engaged in the same manner as John, but they were laughing and carrying on like kids at a shooting gallery on a carnival midway. Larry, the junior medic, and Miguel, the junior weapons sergeant, were engaged in a friendly competition, marking their kills in the sand. John overheard them placing a bet of a hundred dollars to see who could get the most headshots. If only the Iraqi friendly forces had this mindset, this war would already be finished.

But as it was, John couldn't depend on the twenty Iraqi commandos that were supposed to be fighting alongside his team. The commandos were all hunkered down in a shallow ditch nearby, and John was getting frustrated that he had to continuously tell them to return fire. When they did fire, they wouldn't even aim. John guessed that they had a hard time firing on their brothers. Larry and Miguel's game was cut short when they heard John yell, "Everybody, hunker down! I have an aircraft coming in, and we're going to blow this mosque to hell!"

Miguel replied, "Aw, come on, boss. This is fun, and it's a tie game!"

"Shut up and go down the line and make sure all the commandos keep their heads down," John bellowed in answer.

Miguel moved swiftly down the line of entrenched Iraqis, telling them in Arabic to stay near to the ground because Allah was about to make an appearance and shake the earth.

John called in the strike to the aircraft pilot on the radio while Sheb, the senior communications sergeant, stood alongside. Sheb's job was to ensure the radio performed correctly, although this was not necessary, since everyone on the team was crossed-trained in communications. But if ever something went wrong with the radio equipment, the blame fell on Sheb.

John had told Sheb one time that the most unappreciated and taken-for-granted member on the team was the communications sergeant. Set up the radio and make communications a thousand times and nobody notices. However, the *one* time it doesn't work, everyone notices, and you're labeled as a piece of shit. That was why Sheb had become a stickler for details and for proper radio procedure. He had never failed to make communications, and that's the way he wanted it to stay.

The aircraft was close, and everyone could hear it now, even over the continuous rifle fire. The team's senior engineer, Eddie, moved up beside John and Sheb. Eddie could move very swiftly, which was amazing given his size. The guy was six feet, five inches tall and weighed 225 pounds, but he moved like a guy half as large. Even though he was the biggest guy on the team, he was one of the fastest runners. John was happy to have someone like Eddie. Not only was Eddie the strongest person John had ever met, but he dispelled the myth of big guys always being slow.

This was a sore spot for a few of the team members. During a physical training session, John and Eddie would finish a run or a rucksack march well ahead of anyone else, regardless of the distance. On an eight-mile run, John and Eddie would be finished an average of twenty minutes before the next finisher, which was usually Sheb. Several of the younger guys couldn't understand this. How could the biggest guy and the oldest guy be the most physically fit? When asked, John and Eddie would give the same answer: "Effort and attitude!"

Eddie asked, "Hey, John, what type of aircraft we get?"

"An F-16, and he's carrying two five-hundred pounders," John replied.

Eddie rolled over on his back, interlocked his hands behind his head, and stared at the skyline. "This ought to be cool."

The F-16 came in so low that as the aircraft cleared a grove of trees, the treetops swayed in response to the turbulence. The pilot requested final clearance from the ground commander as he approached. John knew this was a requirement for "danger close" runs. He took one last glance around to ensure everyone was ready and, satisfied, granted the pilot's request.

The plane flew right over their heads and immediately banked to the right; the pilot was dead on target. The dome of the mosque disappeared in a blast of dust and concrete fragments. There was no fireball like in the movies, but it was still an impressive show. The blast itself was enough to knock Larry, who was taking pictures, off his feet.

Dumbass!

John just shook his head and chuckled. Well, this was Larry's first combat tour, and there was no better teacher than experience. John was sure that when the next bomb was dropped, Larry would be the first one diving for cover.

When the smoke and dust settled, the soldiers were amazed at the extent of the damage. The dome of the mosque was completely gone, along with the bathroom facility. But the minaret, by some freakish phenomenon, remained standing. They could all see that the minaret had sustained serious damage, but still it defied gravity.

John was about to call the pilot and ask him to make another pass, but before he could key the radio, the pilot's voice crackled over the small speaker to inform John that he was coming around to drop the second of his five-hundred-pound bombs.

Sheb said to John, "You going to say anything to Larry about standing up?"

John looked over to where Larry was crouching. "I think he knows what he did, no point and stating the obvious. Go make sure everyone knows the aircraft is coming back."

The pilot must have been pissed off that the minaret didn't fall, because he came in even lower than before, if that was possible. John swore he saw a treetop torn off by the aircraft's wake.

Once again, the pilot was on the mark. The bomb hit the base of the minaret, and the whole structure was decimated in a split second, leaving nothing but a pile of rubble.

John yelled for all to hear, "Okay. Listen up! Before the dust clears completely we need to use it to mask our movement, cross the field, sweep the whole compound, and assess the damage. Don't take any chances. If you have any doubts, make sure you shoot first, and if you shoot someone, make damn sure you kill him."

Turning to his teammates, John said, "Sheb, you and Larry stay here with five Iraqis and cover us. Eddie, Miguel, and myself will take the remaining fifteen Iraqis and clear the compound. Any questions?"

"No problem, boss," Sheb replied.

"Eddie, you're up front, Miguel, bring up the rear. I'll keep the Iraqis with me in the middle. Let's go."

They moved across the field in a modified V formation, keeping to a quick shuffle all the way to the wall of the compound. They didn't encounter any gunfire. John took this as a good sign; with a little bit of luck, anyone that was left inside the mosque was already dead.

The aircraft's bombs had destroyed large sections of the wall, so finding a place to enter was relatively easy. John was thankful that they didn't have to use the gate located on the street side of the compound. The street stretched straight into the heart of town for eight hundred meters, and there would have been no way to give proper cover fire for anyone that tried to enter or exit the compound through the gate.

"Eddie, you and Miguel take ten Iraqis and clear those two small outbuildings," John said as he went through a hole in the wall.

Portions of the barracks building were still standing, so John took the remaining Iraqis toward it. As they picked their way across the rubble, two men stepped out from behind a standing portion of wall.

John shot both men before they even had an opportunity to raise their rifles. The Iraqi commandos simply stood staring wide-eyed at John. John yelled at them, "Don't look at me! Look for the enemy!" Realizing that the commandos' hesitation and reluctance to fire was likely to get someone killed, John reaffirmed his head position, taking the lead.

John inspected the wounds of his two victims. First one-headshot. John was pleased, figuring why take the time to pump a guy full of rounds when you can just put one in his brain? The next victim was dead from the single shot as well, with the bullet piercing his spinal cord on exit. More proof for the military, John thought, that these 5.56 caliber rounds packed enough punch to get the job done. Lately the higher-ups had been considering moving to 6.8 caliber rounds, but John had always found the 5.56 to perform flawlessly.

John rounded a corner and entered the portion of the barracks building that was still standing. A quick glance told him that there was no threat present—everyone was gone, dead, or buried in the rubble. He could hear gunfire coming from the other end of the compound and knew that Eddie and Miguel were having their own fun.

Eddie entered the first of the two small outbuildings and immediately spotted a man sitting against the wall. He kept his weapon pointed at the man's chest as he stared at the body, thinking, is this guy alive? There was an AK-47 assault rifle lying beside his right leg, but the man didn't make a grab for it.

Miguel came into the room from another door and immediately riddled the sitting man with bullets. Eddie stepped back with a shocked look on his face. Turning to Miguel he said, "Damn it, Miguel, I didn't even know if that guy was already dead or not!"

Miguel smiled while he changed magazines on his weapon. "Well, I would say he's definitely dead now. Let's go clear the other building, and remember what John said: don't hesitate."

This last statement irritated Eddie. Eddie considered himself to be a seasoned veteran, and had never once hesitated in his life. Or had he? He shrugged it off, thinking, no time to think about it now, there's still work to be done.

John moved through the rubble trying to get some kind of estimate on the body count, which was turning into an impossible task because of all the little body parts strewn about. John realized that the Iraqi commandos were having a hard time coping with this—or maybe it was the fact that he had just destroyed a house of Allah.

All of a sudden several explosions rocked the outside the wall of the mosque compound. John pushed the talk button on his radio, calling up Sheb. "Echo One this is Zulu One, what's going on out there?"

"Zulu One this is Echo One, looks like random mortars. Over."

"Echo One this is Zulu One, roger that. We'll be headed your direction in a few minutes. Out."

John tried to raise Miguel. "Bravo Two this is Zulu One. Over."

"Zulu One this is Bravo Two. Over."

"Bravo Two this is Zulu One, wrap it up and move toward the hole in the wall. Over."

"This is Bravo Two, roger, moving now."

Once everyone had assembled at the wall, John received a head count and a sensitive items check. Once accountability was 100 percent, he led the way through the wall.

Just as he stepped through the hole he was lifted off his feet and slammed back against the wall. John knew a mortar had just landed in front of him; he shook his head to clear the cobwebs, got to his feet, and started the movement across the field.

Miguel and Eddie looked at each other and were thinking the same thing: how in the hell did John survive that? Not just surviving the blast from a mortar that landed only a few feet away, but shaking it off and continuing like nothing happened. Luck? Toughness? Or was he just crazy?

The entire element crossed the open field without incident. Several mortars dropped again, but they were a good hundred meters off to the left of the team.

As John returned, Sheb said, "John, the marine commander on the west side of town said he wants to fry this whole area with aircraft and artillery as soon as we can get out of here."

In response, John yelled, "Everyone load up, we're leaving in one minute!"

As the team started to move south, John leaned over and told Sheb to call the marine commander to tell him that they were clear of the area, and that he could commence with the bombardment.

No sooner had Sheb dropped the hand mike of the radio than the first aircraft flew overhead. They all heard and felt the explosion when the first bomb impacted.

"Sheb, pull up in that open field on the left." John said without even looking up from the map he was studying.

A little concerned, Sheb said, "You okay, boss?"

John replied, "Of course. Why wouldn't I be?"

"Two reasons. One is that fucking mortar exploded right in front of your face, and two, you have blood running down the side of your neck."

John touched the side of his neck and felt several pieces of shrapnel lodged under his skin. He looked at Sheb and started to smile. "Just a scratch. And that mortar exploded at least ten feet away."

Sheb just shook his head. "Well, I will say this for you. You're one lucky SOB." Sheb paused a minute and John knew he had something else to say, but he let him take his time. "Boss, not to change the subject, but I need to tell you something about Larry."

The vehicle pulled to a stop in the clearing John had indicated, and he leaned over to Sheb. "What's up?"

Sheb said he would rather wait until they had more time to talk without the chance of being interrupted. John dropped it. He had worked with Sheb for a couple of years and knew when he had something important to discuss, but he also knew Sheb would tell him in his own time.

The team started checking all their equipment, first, to make sure they had everything, and second, to ensure that nothing was damaged. They took their time, pausing to watch the show of aircraft and artillery.

Larry pulled the shrapnel out of John's neck. After finding two pieces, he cleaned John's wounds and taped a strip of gauze to the side of his neck. "You're good, boss." Larry said.

"Thanks," muttered John.

Meanwhile, the marines weren't screwing around; they were pounding the hell out of the whole area.

"Sheb?" John said without taking his eyes off the sky. Another F-16 was making a bombing run, and John never got tired of watching them.

"What's up boss?" Sheb replied, also watching the sky and enjoying the air show and wondering whether people would pay a large amount of money to watch something like this. People already attended air shows all over the world just to watch planes fly around and perform aerial acrobatics. Imagine if those planes were dropping bombs and destroying a town. It would be a sold-out show.

John interrupted Sheb's thoughts. "Call the marines and let the commander know we're returning to the base."

As the team started to load up, John could tell they were disappointed. He knew they wanted to watch the show. Even the Iraqis were having a good time. But John knew that being in charge meant you sometimes had to make decisions that were unpopular.

2

The team drove through the gate of the marine compound and breathed a sigh of relief. It had been a long fight!

The marines had set up a temporary base that was situated ten miles east of Fallujah. John had heard it was a former Iraqi Army base under Saddam's rule. The compound itself was huge. A half-concrete, half-wire wall surrounded the whole compound, which measured a mile long by a half mile wide. The base included dozens of buildings, plus mobile storage containers, tents, and generally all of the equipment one would expect to see in a military compound.

The American team and the Iraqi commandos slept in and worked out of the tent area. Even though they were officially called general purpose tents or GP Larges, the soldiers referred to these as circus tents, because at fifty feet wide and one hundred feet long with three large center poles supporting the entire canvas, they did resemble circus big tops.

The team drove directly to the tent area. Just as the tents came into view, two explosions suddenly rocked their Hummer. Rockets!

Sheb slowed the vehicle down but didn't stop. Brushing dirt and rocks off his uniform, he said to John, "It never ends, does it?"

Spitting dirt out of his mouth, John replied, "Nope."

Pulling up in front of their tent, John got out of the vehicle and started giving orders. "Where's Nadeem?"

Nadeem was the only Iraqi commando that could speak decent English. Between his English and John's ability with the Arabic language, they had been able to communicate quite effectively. This was important because the team had been operating for more than a week without an interpreter who, along with fifty other commandos, had decided to quit.

John addressed the Iraqi. "Nadeem, I need you guys to clean up your equipment, top off your vehicles with fuel, and get some rest. *Faahim?*"

Nadeem replied, "Yes I understand. I must tell you that the soldiers have a new name for you. *Shytaan Ilabyaad.*"

John chuckled, understanding immediately. Nadeem also smiled as he left to relay John's orders to all the commandos.

John gathered the members of the team around the Hummer. "Let's have a quick AAR."

But before John could continue with the after-action review, Eddie asked, "What does *Shytaan Ilabyaad* mean?"

Laughing, John said, "It means The White Devil."

This drew a big laugh from everyone, and Miguel said, "Well, that definitely suits you, with your freaky eyes."

John's eyes were his only distinct physical feature. He wasn't tall, but he wasn't short, although some people said that he appeared taller than his five feet, ten inches. He wasn't overly muscular, but he couldn't be described as thin either. His hair was neither dark nor light in color. He was the most forgettable person you would ever meet—except for his eyes. When people attempted to describe him it usually went, "Remember that guy with the weird eyes?" Those eyes had been described as silver. Others would say they were a bright gray, and still others had called them smoky. No matter how they were described, though, John's eyes always drew the attention of others.

For the next thirty minutes the team discussed what they had done over the last twelve hours—how many people they had killed, what they could have done better, and how the Iraqis had performed. John would occasionally glance at Larry throughout the discussion. Larry never said a word. He added nothing to the discussion and just sat there staring at the ground between his feet continuously. This was odd behavior for an AAR, which was an open-format type of discussion in which everyone was encouraged to participate. Even the lowest ranking guy might have observed something during the operation that may need discussing or changing. The observation could be something as simple as, "When we were crossing the open area we were bunched up. We need to concentrate on maintaining a five-meter spread between every person to avoid a mortar killing more than one person." Despite the casual atmosphere, Larry hardly so much as raised his head.

After the AAR, John watched as the marines started filtering back from the operation. He said, "We need to get everything cleaned up, get vehicles topped off, and conduct another sensitive items check. Sheb, I need you to set up the PSC-5 satellite radio so we can send a sit-rep back to Baghdad. Eddie, check on the Iraqis and make damn sure they clean their weapons."

The team broke up into different directions and started the recovery process. John and Sheb started to set up the radio together so they could file their situation report when Sheb said, "Can I talk to you now boss, about Larry?"

"Let me hear it," John replied as he uncurled the power cables for the laptop.

"Remember when the mortars started coming in on us near the mosque?"

"Yes, I seem to remember that!" John said with a little chuckle.

Sheb opened the antenna and pointed it in a seemingly random direction. As a former communications guy, John knew that the antenna had to be set at a certain azimuth and elevation to hit the satellite. Most people had to use a compass to get it right, but not Sheb. He managed to hit the satellite the first time, every time, and John couldn't remember him ever using a compass.

Sheb continued. "After the mortars started coming in, Larry got down in the ditch with some of the commandos and never came out until you came back across the field from clearing the mosque compound. I think he's scared."

John already suspected something was bothering Larry from his silence during the AAR. Granted, they just got finished with twelve straight hours of fighting. His team had just seen more direct combat in one day than most soldiers experience in a twenty-year military career. That kind of intense combat could screw with anybody's head.

John replied, "I'll talk to him."

Eddie came walking up just as John and Sheb finished the sit-rep, a worried look on his face.

"Boss, the Iraqis are acting up again. I think some of them want to quit and go back to Baghdad."

"Fuck!" John replied while he stormed toward the tent that housed the Iraqi commandos.

John entered the tent and yelled for Nadeem. Nadeem was arguing with several other soldiers, and by the look of his face he was as mad and frustrated as John was. He came over to John and started to explain the problem. "It seems some of the commandos feel uncomfortable about the way the fighting is going. The Iraqi commander has convinced them to quit and follow him back to Baghdad."

John hung his head and took a deep breath. He remembered how only a week ago eighty-three total commandos had accompanied the Americans. But half the commandos quit as soon as word came that they were deploying from Baghdad to Fallujah to fight the terrorists. Over the following week even more Iraqis quit until they had only twenty soldiers left, despite John's encouraging motivational speeches.

Those speeches had included all the reasons a soldier is a soldier: duty, patriotism, country, God, and so on. John even went so far as to tell them that they were the best soldiers in Iraq and must set an example for all Iraqi soldiers to follow. But now, John didn't take this approach. He was pissed off that Americans were more willing to fight for Iraq than Iraqis themselves.

He snapped at Nadeem, "Tell all the commandos to come over here because I got something to say to them."

The commandos gathered around John, expecting another motivational speech. But they were noticeably shocked when John said simply, "I'm tired of you guys whining. If you want to quit, go right ahead. Everybody who wants to quit, run and hide, or act like a pussy, go to the other side of the tent. Those who want to continue to fight with me and stand up for your own independence, stay here."

At first no one moved, so John yelled, "Let's go! Move! Quitters move over to the other side of the tent. *Bisuraah*! Quickly!"

The Iraqi commander clearly showed his intent by being the first to walk across the tent, and for a minute it appeared he would be the only one to do so. But after a moment, nine more crossed to the other side of the tent and joined the commander. This left John standing with only ten commandos—nine Kurds and one Arab. No big shocker there.

John wasn't finished. He looked at the remaining ten guys and said, "Make damn sure you want to stay and fight because if you want to quit, do it now!"

Nobody moved.

Nadeem spoke up. "Everyone standing here will fight with you."

"Okay. Nadeem, you are now in charge. Make sure everyone moves their gear to this side of the tent, and I'll make sure the quitters are moved to another tent."

The team of Americans watched this whole exchange. After Nadeem and the remaining Iraqis started moving their equipment, Eddie and Sheb approached John and Eddie said, "Is ten enough?"

John replied, "Yes. I need you, Sheb, and Miguel to find space in another tent. Get these quitters out of my sight."

"Roger that boss." They hurried to their tasks.

John looked toward the corner of the tent and saw Larry sitting on his bunk, staring at his feet. Might as well handle this problem too, he thought.

He sat down on the cot next to Larry and, having never been known for his sensitivity, said, "What's the matter with you?"

Larry replied without lifting his head. "I can't stand the mortars and rockets. They been falling all day and I start shaking every time one drops. I feel that I have no power over them. I have no problem with anything else; it's just the mortars and rockets."

John, still fuming from his confrontation with the Iraqis, realized that he should have calmed down a few minutes before he confronted Larry, but he was running short on sympathy and he just didn't care. "You're right, a mortar could fall out of the sky anytime and kill you, and it's pure chance on where they will land. You have to deal with it."

This time Larry did look up, "A mortar exploded right in front of your face. How are you dealing with it?"

"There's nothing a person can do when the mortars start falling but hide in a bunker, and since that is not an option for us, you have to shrug it off and continue on." John paused for minute to allow Larry a few minutes to think about what he said, but secretly he knew Larry was finished.

John had seen it before throughout the last couple of years. Many people were just now being forced to learn to deal with the brutality of combat. Nobody was above the reality and fear of death. It didn't matter who you were—the biggest guy, the strongest, or the best trained. Until you came face-to-face with real fighting, and death was biting at your ass, you wouldn't know what your reaction would be.

Larry spoke so softly John had to strain to hear him. He said, "I can't sleep in this tent. There's no overhead cover to stop the mortars or rockets."

"Larry, things are not going to get any better. They may even get worse, so if you're having a hard time coping now, what's going to happen the next time we're out on the street and all hell breaks loose?"

John paused. "I can't have you become a liability during a fire fight. Do you understand what that means?" John was having a hard time keeping his cool. He had no sympathy for Larry. He expected quitters from the Iraqis, but not from a Green Beret!

"Yes, I understand, Sergeant." Larry went back to looking at the floor.

John thought for a minute. "Here's what I'm going to do. Tonight you'll sleep in the bunker area on the north side of the base. I'll let the Command know that they need to arrange transportation for you back to Baghdad, where you'll return to the team house and join the other half of the team. Okay?"

"Thank you, Sergeant."

Miguel had returned to the tent and was waiting off to the side for John and Larry to finish their conversation. When John stood up, Miguel walked over to him and said, "Just wanted you to know, the Iraqi commandos that quit have been moved into the last tent in this row, and Eddie and Sheb are outside working on the truck."

John walked outside with Miguel and the two met Eddie and Sheb. John briefed them on the situation. "Larry's lost it. He's going to move to the bunker area tonight, and I'm going to send him back to Baghdad. I need to know if any of you three have any problems. We are down to four Americans and ten Iraqis; I can't have anybody quitting during a firefight. Eddie?"

Smiling, Eddie said, "The only problem I have is I'm not getting any pussy."

The guys started laughing at this and John said, "What about you two guys?"

Sheb said, "I'm with you, boss."

Miguel sighed. "Pussy would be nice."

This brought another round of laughter and started the wisecracks flowing.

Once again John thought about the different ways in which people dealt with combat, and there was no doubt in his mind that laughter was the best cure.

The guys were taking some humorous jabs at John, especially about the mortar that almost killed him, when John said, "It was the bubble."

This surprised the other three. They all asked, together, "What's the bubble?"

John proceeded to tell the story.

"It all started over a religious debate when I was the senior commo guy on ODA 453, and ..."

3

El Paso, Texas: Two years earlier

The team sat on the ground leaning back against their parachute packs, waiting for the helicopter. John was excited—he had never parachuted out of a civilian helicopter before. Any jump from a helicopter was fun to begin with, but a new or different jump was enough to bring back the initial excitement one got from being at Airborne School.

With the parachutes already donned and the Jumpmaster already finished with the JMPIs—jumpmaster pre-inspections—there was nothing to do but sit around and wait for the aircraft.

John sat beside Tim, poking fun at his size. Tim was so big that the parachute had to be extended to its maximum length, yet he was still barely able to fit in it.

John said, "You know, these parachutes have a weight limit."

Tim gave a chuckle. "Fuck you," he said.

John replied, grinning, "You're so big, I don't think the pilot can even take off with you aboard."

"Fuck you, you anorexic bastard," said Tim.

"I think when your parachute opens, the suspension lines will snap under the weight and you'll plummet to the ground."

Tim retorted, "You're so skinny, you don't have enough weight for your chute to even open, and you'll burn in."

John said, "I think today you'll be a dirt dart."

Tim said, "So how does it feel to know you're going to die today?"

The team members who had not been sitting on the ground had gathered around during this good-natured ribbing. They were all laughing at the exchange between Tim and John—except for Holland.

Holland was an extremely religious guy who always thought it necessary to quote scripture or talk about God, no matter the situation.

John remembered a time when all of them, including Holland, had been in a strip club. After watching naked women dance and parade around for five hours, drinking enough beer to fill a small lake, and spending a month's wages, the team left the club.

Sitting in the car getting ready to leave, Holland had said drunkenly, "That place is a nest of evil. It is the devil's playground."

Before anyone could reply to this statement, Holland's head had tilted back against the seat as he passed out.

"You two don't have to worry about the jump. God will look after you and protect you," Holland now said.

Tim looked at John and rolled his eyes as if to say, here we go again!

"Yeah, right," John said. He remembered the strip club and wondered whether Holland would ever tell his wife that he had spent a whole afternoon watching naked women and drinking beer. John doubted it, and he had nothing but disdain for a hypocrite.

Tim threw gas on the fire, saying, "Holland, do you know what God is? He is the result of the biggest con game in the history of human events."

Flustered, Holland answered, "I know God exists and that he's with me always."

John rolled over on his side and looked directly at Holland. "You do not *know* that God exists. Nobody *knows* if God exists. You may believe with all your heart and have all the faith in the world, but you don't *know*. The only way to know for sure is to die, and if you're wrong, you still won't know because your consciousness will die with you."

"So, smart guy! What do you think happens when you die?" Holland asked.

"Nothing, you're just dead," John answered.

"Come judgment day, you two will have to answer for your sins," Holland retorted.

"What if you're wrong?" Tim asked.

Holland replied, "I'm not wrong."

"I'll concede that there may be a God," Tim began, "but will you concede that God may have been created by man in response to events that couldn't be explained scientifically at the time?"

"What does that mean?" Holland asked.

Tim answered, "I'm saying that throughout history, man has always had an inherent need to understand everything around him, and when he can't understand something he tends to use God as an answer, excuse, or scapegoat—because I think man, by his nature, is weak"

Holland replied, "You guys will definitely burn in hell."

John jumped back in the debate. "If there is a heaven and hell, I hope I go to hell."

Holland looked shocked. "You don't really mean that."

John shrugged. "Every place I've been, every country I worked in or visited, and every culture I've seen, the people all believe they're going to heaven. The Muslims think they're right; the Christians think they're right; everyone thinks they're right and everyone else is wrong. So, since everybody on the planet believes they're going to heaven, I expect the devil will be feeling kind of lonely and would welcome some company. I bet he even puts me in charge of something—hopefully the concubines."

This last comment brought loud laughter from the rest of the team.

Holland said, "I believe what I believe."

Tim came back with, "Holland, did you know that seven hundred years ago everybody on the planet believed and was one hundred percent certain the Earth was flat? It would have been impossible to convince anyone of that time period that the Earth was round, and look how that turned out." Tim was on roll. "It was only one hundred twenty-five years ago that people believed it was impossible to make a machine fly, and today there is one coming to pick us up and take us for a ride."

Holland's response was simple. "And your point is?"

"I'm just saying that throughout history, man has believed in a lot of things that turned out not to be true. It's always good to keep an open mind. Nothing wrong with believing in a supreme being that may or may not exist, but a man of your intelligence has to admit that maybe he's wrong."

After Tim finished, the members of the team who had been watching this exchange stood up and got ready because they could hear the helicopter coming.

John looked at Holland and said for all to hear, "If God is real, he has the chance to kill me on this jump and still not reveal himself because everyone will call it an accident. In fact, I'll yell, 'Fuck God!' as I'm exiting the helicopter. We'll see what your God does."

After this declaration, the team sergeant grabbed John by the arm and led him off to the side. He instructed John to knock it off because a lot of people were getting freaked out. John simply shrugged and said, "Yes, sergeant."

The first six jumpers lined up as the helicopter slowly descended to the ground. John watched from a hundred meters away; he was set to jump on the second lift of the aircraft with the last five guys of the team, including Holland.

Holland broke from the group and ran up to the team sergeant who was slotted to jump on the first lift. John couldn't hear what they were talking about, but he could make an accurate guess as to the content of the conversation.

After a few minutes, Tim was taken out of the first lift and was replaced with Holland. Tim walked slowly back to where John was standing, shaking his head and cussing to himself the whole way.

"Well?" John asked as Tim approached.

"Holland said he didn't want to jump with you." Tim said.

"Imagine that." John laughed.

Tim looked at John, "How come it's always the religious guys that do the most complaining?"

John thought for a minute. "I think you said it before—they're weak."

There were no incidents or injuries during the jump, although some were visibly relieved when it was safely over.

While loading the chutes into the back of a truck, John turned to Holland and said, "He had his chance."

Holland said, "God doesn't work that way."

"I thought you would say that," John replied. "Let me tell you why God didn't do anything. God can't touch me because the devil has a protective bubble around me."

"So, you admit it? You sold your soul to the devil?" Holland stated, confidently.

John laughed. "Well I tried once, but the devil said, 'Why should I pay for something that I already own?'"

And thus "the legend of the bubble" was born and continued to grow through the next couple of years. On the evening of March 18, 2003—about six months after the parachuting exercise—the team was located in Kuwait getting ready to launch into Iraq. All the rehearsals were finished, everything was packed up, and nothing was left to do but wait.

John was told that their team would be the first Americans to enter Iraq, along with some teams that would drive across the border between Jordan and Iraq while his team was landing in the desert south of Nasiriyah.

Tim would be driving the Toyota with John riding shotgun. John was also the designated vehicle commander, by virtue of rank. In the back seat sat Jerry, an Air Force tactical controller whose purpose was to control aircraft in the event the team needed combat air support once inside Iraq.

Tim and John sat relaxing in the truck while waiting in line to drive into their transport helicopter when suddenly Tim said, "Holy shit! Look at this." He pointed at the vehicle's odometer.

John leaned over and looked. The odometer read 666 miles. John looked at Tim and started laughing. "Well, that's interesting. Looks like the bubble."

Tim said, "Bubble my ass, this is freaking me out. I'm going to drive around for a while so this thing changes."

John leaned back in his seat and said, "Whatever."

John explained to Jerry what "the bubble" meant as they drove around the compound. After several minutes of driving in circles, the team sergeant finally stopped them and told them to quit wasting gas and to get back in line and ready to load into the back of the helicopter.

John was half asleep. He asked Tim, "Did the odometer change yet?"

"No, it didn't, it must be stuck." Tim said hopefully. Tim had never been a religious man, but sometimes things happened that made a person stop and think.

The whole team—gear, truck, and all—loaded into the back of the Pave Low MH53s transport helicopter. They were ready at last to be air landed into the desert south of Nasiriyah, Iraq.

The flight itself was an adventure. All six helicopters flew west into Saudi Arabia, where they conducted an in-flight refuel. During the refueling process, the helicopter would tilt back while continuing to fly forward, its nose pointed skyward. This way it was able to be refueled without the rotor blades interfering.

The Toyota trucks had been backed into the helicopters and ratcheted to rings that were imbedded in the aircraft floor. With only a couple inches of clearance on both sides of the Toyota, the only place for the team to ride during flight was in the cab of the truck. While the chopper was refueling, the guys inside the trucks were staring right at the ground. All they could do was hope the ratchet straps wouldn't break—if they did, the Toyota would shoot out the back of the helicopter. The Toyota was a tough truck, but nobody believed it would survive a thousand-foot freefall. Tim brought this fact up during the refueling process.

John smiled. "If the straps break and we fall to the earth all you have to do is wait until the truck is about to hit the ground and then step out. Don't worry; you're inside the bubble now."

Tim had to laugh. "Yeah, I'm sure jumping out of the truck just before impact will work," he said. "You are crazy!"

The plan was for three of the helicopters to land, allow the Toyotas to drive off, and then take off again. The other three choppers would then follow the same drill.

Jerry was listening to the aircraft frequency that the pilots were using. He informed the others, "We're one minute from landing."

Before John or Tim could reply, Jerry said excitedly, "One of the helicopters crashed!"

There was silence inside the cab of the truck until finally Tim said, "What are we going to do?"

John realized that they couldn't do anything and said, "Well, it ain't this chopper. We do exactly as we rehearsed—when our chopper lands, we drive two hundred meters, stop and set up the commo wire, and move to the rally point. From there we'll find out what's going on."

Tim and John drove off their helicopter without any problems. As they cleared the rotor wash, Tim said, "The odometer just changed to 667."

All three men looked at each other and at the same time said, "The bubble."

4

"So 'the legend of the bubble' continues," Sheb said, laughing, "But I know there's more to the bubble story than you're telling. You have to tell the story about the ambush incident in Nasiriyah."

"Nah, maybe I'll tell you some more bubble stories later," John replied, and then added, "It's getting late. You guys make sure Larry gets moved and settled in at the bunker area. Find out if there are any aircraft leaving for Baghdad tonight, and if so get Larry on one, then get some rack time. I'm going to talk to the marine commander, see if they got anything going on."

John walked to the circus tent occupied by the marines and set up for briefings and planning. When he entered, the marine commander said, "I'm glad you're here Sergeant Smith. We got something for you."

The marine commander briefed John on what they were planning to do that night. "Sergeant, we're going to send a company-sized element into this area of southern Fallujah." He pointed to the map that was laid out on the floor and paused to allow John to get himself oriented on the map. When John nodded, the marine commander continued. "Our plan is to sweep this area in the hopes of pushing the terrorists north into a blockade of tanks. There is a mosque located here." Once again the commander pointed to the map and gave John the time to write down the grid location.

"Sir, you want us to check out the mosque?" John asked.

"We think it is being used for a weapons depot and recruiting center. We also have imagery for you." Commander handed John a set of three pictures.

John sat down on a cot to study the pictures, and noticed that there appeared to be no wall around the mosque. This was unusual, although not unheard of; most mosques were walled-in compounds. The dome and the minaret were present, but it appeared that they were in disrepair.

"Sir, when do you want to leave?" John asked.

"We leave from here at 0200 local. Will you be ready for that?"

"Yes, sir," John replied without looking up from the pictures he was studying. He glanced at his watch—2000. Six hours away, plenty of time. He went back to studying the pictures and the map.

The marines spent the next four hours planning out all the details of their operation, and then they briefed all their soldiers on every detail of the plan. John sat in on all the planning and the briefings, giving him the details he needed to refine his own plan, which he would give to his guys and the remaining commandos.

John woke Sheb up at 0100 and gave him a quick summary of their mission.

"I need you to wake everybody up and get them ready. I want to brief you guys on the plan at 0130, and then I'll brief the commandos at 0145. Okay?" John said while rubbing his eyes.

"No problem, boss. Did you get any sleep?" Sheb asked, concerned.

John shrugged him off. "I'll take a magic pill. In fact, make sure all you guys take one. I don't want anyone dozing during this."

Sheb got up from his bunk and started walking over to wake up Eddie and Miguel, but he paused, looked over his shoulder at John, and said, "By the way boss, Larry flew back to Baghdad about two hours ago."

John nodded, but didn't say anything. Good riddance!

The team gathered around the Toyota truck at 0130 to hear the operations plan. Sheb loved John's briefings; they never followed the Army format. His were quick and to the point. John never covered the details, or what other people call the 'what ifs.' He just figured you should know them.

John started his briefing. "Take a look at the map and the photos. I've marked our objective. The marines are going to sweep this whole area." John pointed at the map and continued, "We will move on line with the marines, along their right flank. When we get to the mosque we will storm it. Miguel and Eddie, you guys will take the Hummer and five Iraqis and try to get in the right side of the Mosque. Sheb, you and I will take the Toyota and five Iraqis and try to enter someplace on the left." John paused for questions.

Eddie asked, "Where are the doors?"

John replied, "That's the problem. I don't know. If we come in from both sides someone should find a door. Whoever finds an entry point, call the other team and let them know. Don't forget to leave a couple of Iraqis outside for security and to watch the vehicles."

After waiting for more questions, John continued. "Once we secure the mosque we will stand by and wait for the marine commander to call. He said they may have a follow-up mission for us. Sheb, make sure we have the same crypto and frequency as the marines."

"Got, it boss," Sheb replied.

"Any more questions?" John asked, looking at all their faces.

Miguel asked, "Rules?"

John looked at him, and Miguel instantly knew he asked a stupid question. But Miguel also knew there were no such things as stupid questions, only stupid people. It was always better to ask a stupid question than to be a stupid person.

John smiled. "Kill everyone, and don't take any chances. If anyone has a problem with that, remember this: these bastards just killed, burned, and hung four Americans." He looked at Eddie and asked, "Eddie, you're kind of quiet. Anything wrong?"

Eddie said, "Fucking Sheb woke me up while I was having a wet dream!"

Everyone busted up laughing and John said, "Don't worry Eddie. We'll get you laid soon enough. You guys know what to do; get everything ready while I go brief the Iraqis."

At 0200, all the marines were ready to go. The team sat waiting in their vehicles; everyone was wired and ready for action thanks to a wonderful little pep pill called Adderall.

The movement started at 0210. The team was located in the rear of the convoy as they left the safety of the compound. As the entire convoy moved into a staging area in southern Fallujah, the mortars started to fall.

Sheb looked over at John. "I guess they know we're coming."

"Let's break off and move to the right of the marines," John replied.

As the team got on line and were waiting for the marine commander to give them the green light to take the mosque, two Hummers pulled up behind the Toyota. John looked in the mirror and said, "Who the fuck is this?"

"Looks like Chief Horner and his guys," Sheb said, exiting the vehicle.

John mumbled something under his breath. Sheb didn't catch it, but it sounded something like, "assholes."

Eddie came running up to John, out of breath. "Boss, Chief Horner and three of his crew are here."

"Thanks Eddie," John said, walking toward the newcomers. Chief Horner, a Special Forces Warrant Officer, had been in the area collecting intelligence. John understood the importance of intelligence collection, but he didn't think that they had the proper financing or equipment for that mission. But most of all he just plain didn't like Horner, who looked like a seventy-year-old man and had a gut that would put any professional beer drinker to shame. In John's opinion, Horner's disgraceful appearance was an embarrassment.

John approached the chief. "Good morning, chief. What are you guys doing out here?"

Horner replied with his typical arrogant attitude. "We're meeting two guys that are supposed to give us some information, and we need to use your interpreter."

"Under different circumstances that wouldn't be a problem, but as it happens we don't have an interpreter," John said, smiling.

"You mean to tell me that you guys have been operating out here for over a week without an interpreter?" Horner said with disbelief.

John nodded.

"Then how have you been communicating with your soldiers? Who does your speaking?" Horner asked.

John simply said, "I do."

Horner gave a start. "That's hard for me to believe."

John just shrugged his shoulders. He could care less if Horner didn't believe him. If he had said it once, he had said it a hundred times: "If you're not going to believe me, don't fucking ask!"

Sheb yelled in their direction, "Boss, we just got the call to take the mosque!"

"Okay, everybody load up," John said, and turning toward Chief Horner, he added, "We have to roll, and I'd appreciate it if you guys would stay back, out of the way."

Horner said, "We'll come with you."

John turned abruptly and said, "No! Normally I would welcome the help, but you guys have not trained with us, and I don't want to worry about someone else on the mission who may do something different than we're used to."

John didn't wait for the chief to answer. He jumped in the vehicle with Sheb and said, "Let's go."

"I'm proud of you boss, thought for a minute you were going to kick his ass," Sheb said, chuckling.

John was checking his weapon one more time. Without looking up he said, "I always said that guy was an idiot. I know a lot of people think he's super smart, but he's an idiot to come out here without an interpreter when he can't speak the language. The only reason he's even out here is so he can brag and say, 'I was in Fallujah!'"

With that they dropped the subject, and John got on the team radio. "Listen up everyone. The mosque is around this corner and five hundred meters down the street on the left side. Everyone ready?"

Eddie: "Roger."

Miguel: "Roger."

Sitting beside John, Sheb echoed: "Roger."

The team rounded the corner and came face-to-face with the mosque. John was already out and moving before Sheb could even stop the vehicle. There was no way Sheb was going to let John have all the fun this time; he sprang out of the vehicle and ran to catch up with him.

John turned to Sheb and said, "We need to hold up a minute, give Eddie and Miguel a minute to get set and wait for the slow-ass Iraqis."

Sheb pointed to the left. "Looks like a door, down this little alley."

John patted Sheb on the back. "Let's go!"

John stacked on the side of the door and glanced over his shoulder to make sure the Iraqis were with them. Satisfied, he tried the door.

It was locked!

Just then they heard gunfire from the other side of the mosque.

Eddie's voice broke on the radio, "Zulu One this is Charlie One, we found an entry point and some bad guys. Over.

John replied, "This is Zulu One, we are on our way. Out."

He turned to Sheb. "Sheb, keep one Iraqi with you and watch this door. I'll take the other two with me and go help out." John grabbed two commandos and started to move to the other side of the street.

Not saying anything, Sheb took a knee and kept his rifle trained on the door. He looked beside him, recognized Ahmed, and said, "*Jaahiz?*"

Ahmed replied in English, "Yes, I'm ready."

Sheb muttered under his breath, "We'll see about that."

On the inside, Sheb was disappointed to find himself in a covering position again. He wanted to be in the direct action this time. But he couldn't get mad at John, because he understood why the team sergeant should be on the objective.

Sheb also understood that most people clear a room and then stand around waiting for something. Nobody knows what they're waiting for, they just stand around. John wasn't like that; he kept everything flowing nice and smooth.

The two men heard the door start clanking. Someone was coming out!

It had to be a bad guy because Sheb could hear gunfire coming from inside the mosque, so he knew the team hadn't finished clearing it yet.

The door burst open. Sheb took only a split second to confirm that these were bad guys. He opened up with semi-automatic fire dropping the first two guys that came through, but this did not stop the flow. People continued to pour out the door, and several were now firing back at Sheb and Ahmed.

Sheb tried to control his rate of fire but the alley they were in was filling up with people fast. He ducked into a crouching position and started moving sideways, knowing that it was harder to hit a moving target. He knew Ahmed was firing, but judging by the sound he was firing on automatic. Sheb knew from experience that you could not place accurate fire while on automatic, even from the short distance of ten meters now separating them from the enemy. The first shot might find a target, but it was almost impossible to maintain control of the gun after that, and the rest of the rounds would go high.

As Sheb continued to move sideways, he could hear and sense that Ahmed had stopped firing, probably out of bullets. Then Sheb felt a blow to his stomach that felt like a prizefighter had punched him. He went down to one knee, having difficulty breathing. He thought he was still firing, but couldn't be sure. Everything went black.

5

"Sheb? Sheb? Can you hear me?" John rubbed his knuckle into Sheb's chest, trying to elicit some type of response.

Eddie leaned over John's shoulder. "Is he going to make it?"

Just then Sheb's eyes popped open.

He was confused; his eyes slowly came into focus, and he recognized John leaning over him. The last thing he could remember was the fight in the alley.

"How you feeling?" John asked.

Sheb looked around and realized he was inside the mosque lying on his back with everyone gathered around him. Then the pain in his stomach hit him. He grimaced, looked up at John, and asked, "How bad is it?"

With a serious look on his face, John said, "I'm going to be brutally honest with you. You been shot in the stomach and it left a huge hole. We got most of your entrails back in, but it doesn't look good."

With frightened eyes, Sheb said, "John? Just tell my wife I love her."

Everyone started laughing, and Sheb looked around at all of them, confused and angry. He thought, here I'm about to die, and they're laughing at me. Sheb thought he must be delirious, or maybe even dead.

John said laughing, "Tell her yourself. The bullet never penetrated your body armor. You're not dying, but you're going to have one hell of bruise to show off."

Sheb sat up slowly. The pain was still intense. Looking down at his stomach, Sheb could see no blood but could see the beginnings of a world-class bruise. He looked at John, scowling. "You asshole, that wasn't even close to being funny."

Sheb started getting dressed, and John gave him the full story. The team had moved through the mosque and had killed four guys on the inside, but the remaining bad guys started to retreat through the back door. The team pursued them and got into the alley just in time to see Sheb go down. They entered the alley and killed the remaining enemies. John further explained that Sheb's kill count had reached six, leaving only two alive by the time the team had arrived. The bullet that hit Sheb in the body armor had knocked the air out of him and he had passed out.

Sheb asked, "What about Ahmed?"

John dropped his head. "He took a bullet in the face and was killed instantly."

"Damn it," Sheb said, shaking his head.

John added, "He fought beside you, and it looks like he fought good. He had emptied one magazine and was in the process of changing magazines when he got nailed. The other Iraqis are seeing to his body."

Sheb replied, "It's hard losing the ones who will actually fight."

John said, "Yeah. I'm going outside to see how things are. You going to be all right?"

Putting his vest back on, Sheb replied, "I'm fine. I may be a little slow for a couple of days, but I'll make it. Thanks to the bubble."

John, walking out, looked over his shoulder and said, "Come on outside when you're ready."

There were two more Hummers in the street when John walked back out—Chief Horner and his crew had pulled up. John went to his vehicle, where Miguel was monitoring the radio. He asked, "Anything on the radio?"

"No," Miguel said. "How's Sheb?"

"He'll be fine. Let's pull the vehicles off the road, put them tighter against the mosque."

After John had moved the Toyota into the mouth of the alley, Chief Horner walked up to him. "Looks like you guys had a few problems."

"We have it under control," John said patiently, "What are you guys doing over here?"

"One of our intelligence sources is here. We need you to translate for us," the chief said.

"Chief, my language skills are limited. I can't handle an in-depth interview. Now, if there are some basic questions you want me to ask, that I can do."

Sheb walked out of the mosque and immediately started to reposition the Iraqis into a better defensive posture. He told Miguel to rotate the fifty-caliber machine gun so it pointed down the street, and explained the sectors of fire to him. Sheb walked up to John and said, "I'll watch the radio."

John smiled, glad to have Sheb back in the game. "Sheb, I'm going to go talk to this guy for the chief. Have Eddie go through the weapons cache inside the mosque and see if there is anything we can use."

John walked over to where the chief's source was sitting and introduced himself. After the typical Iraqi pleasantries and greetings, John turned to the chief. "What do you want to ask him?"

The chief said he wanted to know if the guy had any information. John just shook his head; they all had information.

John asked the question, and the Iraqi started rambling a million miles an hour.

Stopping the Iraqi, John explained to him that he must talk slowly or else he couldn't understand him. But it was no use—yet again the Iraqi started talking way to fast for John to understand. Getting frustrated, he turned to the chief. "He's talking too fast and I can't follow him. If you have a specific question to ask, I can try that."

Chief Horner nodded. "Ask him, 'What is the basic terrorist cell structure of the insurgency in western Fallujah?'"

John just laughed. "I have no idea on how to say that; I was thinking more simple than that, like, 'Where do you live?'"

The chief looked at John and said, "Maybe this can wait until another day."

"That's probably best," John replied, and then added, "He's part of a cell, isn't he?"

The chief explained to John that this man was just a foot soldier in the cell structure of Fallujah, and they had been trying to find out through him who the financiers and the cell leaders were.

John said, "If he's a part of a terrorist cell, why don't you just kill him?"

Chief Horner explained, "These foot soldiers are a dime a dozen. They can be replaced easily; there's an endless supply of jihadists willing to step right in."

John told the chief he was sorry he couldn't be of more help, and started back to where his team was waiting. On the way he thought to himself how he disagreed with the chief's way of thinking. These terrorists, he thought, all want to be known as the most important man in their organization—bragging rights. If a cell leader or financier was killed or captured, then someone else would move up in the organization and become more important. So the foot soldier was the actually the hardest person to replace because he'd have to be vetted, recruited, trained, and started at the bottom. Nobody wanted to be at the bottom of any organization. In this line of thinking, the higher levels in a terrorist cell were the easiest to fill. When you're at the top, there'd be no more putting your ass on the line, and more bragging rights.

John felt that making the street dangerous for the terrorists was the way to beat them. Maybe he was wrong. It just seemed so much easier to kill them, and then you'd know they would never climb the ladder in a terrorist organization, or kill any more people.

Eddie, who was standing by the mosque and waving at him, snapped John out of his thoughts.

"What's up, Eddie?"

"I found six brand new AK-47s and three pistols. Everything else is bombs, mortars, or older stuff," Eddie reported.

"Pass the pistols out to the commandos; make sure Nadeem gets the best one, and put the AK-47s in the back of the Hummer." John paused for a minute, and then added, "Eddie, do we have enough C-4 to blow all the munitions and collapse the mosque?"

Eddie got that little twinkle in his eye and said, "I love the way you think, boss. Let me do some calculations."

John walked to the Toyota where Sheb was monitoring the radio. "Anything going on?"

Sheb yawned. "Nope."

Suddenly the side window of the Toyota shattered, and the report of a rifle shot followed. John and Sheb scrambled to the other side of the Toyota and crouched down behind one of the axles. Grimacing with pain and holding his stomach, Sheb said excitedly, "Damn that was close!"

John didn't reply; he was looking down the street to see where the shot had come from. Another shot sounded, this time in the direction of some of the Iraqis, who were hiding behind an abandoned vehicle. Someone had stuck his head up just a little too high, and the shooter had put a hole through his cap.

John now knew the general location of the shooter. Enemy sniper, and by the looks of his shooting a damn good one. Probably one of the Chechnya snipers that were rumored to be in Fallujah.

The whole team, except Eddie who was inside the mosque, was pinned down. The Iraqi commandos were immobilized too. Even Chief Horner and his guys were hunkered down behind their Hummer.

John keyed his personal radio, disregarding radio procedure. "Miguel where are you?"

"I'm lying behind the Hummer."

"Can you get in the back of the Hummer and grab the sniper rifle and spotting scope?"

"Yes, I think so."

"Good." John gave him the rest of the plan. "Get the sniper rifle and spotting scope and make a dash for the door of the mosque. Come through to this side and I will meet you at the alley door. I'll make a lunge for the alley door. This should distract the sniper and allow you the time you need. You copy?"

"Good copy, I'm ready anytime." Miguel was poised.

John's only signal as he dove for the alley was, "Go!" The sniper got off one shot at John, but the bullet hit the front of the Toyota and imbedded itself into the bumper.

John's distraction worked well. Miguel was sure that the sniper didn't even see him as he quickly grabbed the sniper rifle and the spotting scope, then crossed to the mosque and was through the door in four big bounds. He raced through the interior and bumped into Eddie.

Eddie accompanied Miguel to the alley door, having heard John's plan over the radio. He said, "Boss, I think the sniper is about four hundred meters down the street, to the east."

"Do you have a fix on his position?" John asked.

"No. I know the general area where he's hiding, and I think I know which building he's firing from, but not the exact location."

"Okay Eddie. Do you think you and Miguel can climb the building just beside the mosque, set up in a position, and try a shot?"

Eddie took the sniper rifle from Miguel and slung it across his back, "We'll be set in five minutes."

Eddie and Miguel bolted around the back of the building, and spotting a door Eddie didn't even break stride as he rammed into it with all his weight. The door and frame buckled and groaned under the force of Eddie's shoulder, but held. Miguel knew that any door that could withstand a battering from a guy the size of Eddie was a very well-built door.

Eddie backed up, looked at Miguel, and said, "Together. Ready … go!" They both hurled all their weight at the door, and it collapsed inward, ripping the frame completely out of the wall. Their momentum sent both men sprawling.

Eddie was thankful he had enough sense to land on his stomach to protect the sniper rifle. He was on his feet in seconds. Eddie saw Miguel get up and rub his shoulder. He said, "You all right?"

"I'm fine and so is the spotting scope. Let's find the stairs."

Outside in the alley John waited patiently for the call from Eddie. Meanwhile, Sheb was still crouching behind the tire of the Toyota. John called him. "Sheb, stay where you are-I got a plan."

"Don't worry about me. I'm not about to go anywhere," came the reply.

John chuckled and was about to make a wisecrack when Eddie's voice came on the radio.

"Boss, we are positioned. I can see the entire area."

"Good. Watch the area real close through the scope because the sniper is going to show himself real soon." John then added, "Are you ready?"

"I'm ready."

Suddenly John ran into the street, running fast across the street in a jerky, weaving pattern.

The guys on the roof saw this and were shocked at the suddenness of it. Eddie realized too late that he should have been watching for the sniper instead of watching John sprint across the street. The sniper managed to get off two shots at John before the team leader got to safety around the corner of the building across the street. Eddie had seen movement in a window of a three-story building, but he couldn't be certain it was the sniper.

John yelled to him from across the street, "Well?"

Eddie yelled back, "I'm fairly certain I know which window he's in, but right now I don't have a shot." He turned to Miguel. "This time we keep our eyes glued to the scopes." Miguel nodded.

John didn't hesitate. "Get ready, he's going to shoot again," He radioed. Then he dashed into the street once more.

This time Eddie caught the movement of the enemy sniper and fired a split second before the enemy could get a clean shot at John. Or so he thought. Next to him, Miguel said excitedly, "Direct hit! Right in the chest."

Sheb watched the events from the cover behind the Toyota's tire. John had only been midway across the street when Sheb heard what sounded like two shots. He saw John go down. "Shit!" Sheb yelled as he immediately came out from behind the Toyota to help John. But the leader suddenly sprang to his feet and ran into the alley behind the mosque, then collapsed against the wall. Sheb followed him into the alley. "Boss, are you hit?"

"No, I'm just smoked," John said through gasps of breath. He looked up and saw Miguel and Eddie coming in from the neighboring building.

"We got him, boss," Eddie said.

John stood up and leaned against the wall. "Sheb, go tell everyone the threat is gone."

"Boss, look at your foot," Sheb said.

John looked at his right foot and realized he had lost the heel of his combat boot, and he realized that that was probably why he had stumbled. "I'm going to see if I can find my heel. This is the only pair of boots I have with me, and maybe I can nail it back on."

Sheb just shook his head as he left the alley to inform everyone that they had killed the enemy sniper. As he told the Iraqis to get back to their security positions, he heard John yell from down the street, "I found it!"

Sheb was incredulous at John. He was crazy! He had almost been killed twice, and his only concern was his damn boot heel.

The bubble!

Eddie and Miguel returned to the street and saw that the Iraqis were back in their proper positions. Even Chief Horner and his men were moving about.

Eddie approached John, who was sitting on the ground with his boot off. He had a roll of duct tape and was trying to figure out the best way to reattach the heel.

"Sorry we were a little slow on pinpointing the sniper's location," Eddie apologized.

"Don't worry about it. The sniper's dead, that's all that matters. Take a look at this." John handed the boot heel to Eddie.

Eddie's eyes got wide, and everyone leaned in to get a better look. All eyes saw a bullet lodged in the heel, making it clear to everyone that it was the sniper's shot that had caused John to stumble and fall. John simply took the heel back and begun taping it onto the boot.

Eddie said, "Damn, you're lucky."

John replied with a smile, "Has nothing to do with luck. Thanks to your good shooting and the bubble, I'll live to fight another day."

He finished the taping job and slipped his boot back on. As he was lacing it up he said, "Call the marine commander and tell him the mosque is no longer being used as a mosque, and we're going to blow it up."

Chief Horner walked up behind John just in time to overhear this last exchange.

"Sergeant Smith, you can't blow up this mosque," Chief said immediately.

"Watch me!"

"You guys cleared all the bad guys out of it, and since the mosque is no longer being used as an active fighting position, under the rules of engagement you're not allowed to destroy it," the chief countered.

"Chief, it's not a mosque anymore. I expect it hasn't been used as a mosque for years," John said, maintaining his cool. He thought, for someone that's supposed to be the smartest guy in the unit, Horner sure is stupid!

"You don't know that, and I can't allow this to happen," Horner retorted.

Smiling, John said, "Follow me." He led the way back into the mosque, through the alley, and past the spot where Sheb was almost killed, and where Ahmed wasn't so lucky. The other commandos had done a wonderful job with Ahmed's body, considering the circumstances. They had washed his body with water and wrapped him up with a rug they had found in one of the nearby buildings. The body was now loaded into the back of one of the commandos' trucks.

Chief Horner was astounded at the amount of blood that was splattered on every surface of the alleyway.

"What happened in this alley?" he asked.

John ignored him and led him through the door into the mosque.

Once inside, John saw that Eddie was staying busy by moving boxes of ammunition, stacking mortars, and taking an inventory of all the weapons systems. Eddie watched as John and the chief entered the mosque. John addressed him. "What's the story, Eddie?"

Eddie knew he was referring to the possibility of them blowing up the mosque. He didn't say anything, just gave John a thumbs up.

Now the purpose of John leading Horner into the building became clear. "Take a look Chief, and tell me what you see," John said while, leaning against a wall. John was hopeful the chief would see what he had noticed earlier.

The chief turned to John after taking a look around. "All I see is a bunch of weapons, which still doesn't authorize you to destroy this mosque."

John walked over to the door where they entered; it was time to give the chief a cultural lesson.

He pointed to the doorframe. "This door was installed in the last couple of years. You can tell by the steel frame that has all the paint on it. Newer bolts and screws that have no rust on them."

John looked over his shoulder, but the chief still had a blank look on his face. Still patient, John said, "This door was installed in the qibla wall."

John continued to explain that mosques are built according to divine guidance and not specific patterns. However, he explained that there are a few mandatory elements that must be built into a mosque. One of these is a wall that clearly indicates the direction of Mecca. This wall cannot contain any windows or doors, and is called the qibla.

John finished by saying, "If they installed a door into the qibla, that means this mosque is no longer being used as a mosque; it has been decommissioned, for a lack of a better word. Now it's considered as just another building."

John could tell that Chief Horner finally understood.

Sheb walked into the mosque and reported, "Boss, the marine commander said if you want to blow up the mosque it's your call."

John didn't hesitate to look over at Eddie and say, "Wire it. Five minute fuse."

Eddie gave out a yelp of joy and said, "I need thirty minutes and someone to help me."

"I'll go get Miguel to help you," John said, then turned to Horner. "Are we done, Chief?"

Chief Horner stormed out of the mosque without saying another word, and John followed him. The chief went straight to his vehicle and told his crew to load up. John watched them drive off to the south.

Sheb walked up beside John and said, "I'm glad that asshole is gone."

"You and me both," John replied with a sigh of relief before yelling to Miguel, "Hey, Miguel! Go inside and help Eddie wire the place."

When Miguel got inside he could tell that Eddie was well into rigging the explosives. The engineer looked up from what he was doing and said, "Go out to the Hummer and get the rest of the C-4."

"How much?" Miguel asked.

Without looking up Eddie said, "All of it!"

Miguel walked outside and looked in the Hummer for the explosive. When he found sixty pounds of C-4 he thought, all of it, huh? This is going to be big.

The weapons sergeant came back into the mosque to find Eddie using a steel bar to break concrete blocks out of the wall.

"What are we doing?" Miguel asked eagerly.

Eddie stopped what he was doing and showed Miguel the pile of weapons that were already wired.

"All the weapons are ready for detonation. Once the C-4 explodes it will, in turn, cause the bombs, artillery shells, and mortar rounds to explode. This should cause enough heat to ignite and destroy all the smaller ammunition, which I've stacked below the bigger stuff." Eddie continued, passion in his voice, "The explosion of this entire pile will cause the support structure behind it to fail, which will cause this side of the dome roof to collapse under its own weight."

Together they walked over to the wall where Eddie had started digging out concrete blocks. Eddie explained to Miguel, "We need to dig a big enough hole in this wall to pack the remaining C-4. This wall is not only part of the dome, but it's also part of the minaret structure. In theory, and if my calculations are correct, by exploding this simultaneously with the weapons pile the minaret wall will be weakened enough that the whole tower should fall onto the roof of the dome and collapse what remains. When it's finished, there should be a beautiful pile of rubble; a fitting grave for all the bad guys we killed."

Miguel was impressed and had only one question, "Why don't we stack the bodies on the explosives?"

"Human flesh is too light; the force of the explosion would fling body parts everywhere. By stacking them on the opposite side, they won't be affected by the explosion but will be buried nicely under several tons of rubble."

"Cool!" Miguel said. "What do you want me to do?"

Eddie handed him a steel bar. "Make the hole I started bigger."

In less than twenty minutes, Eddie and Miguel had everything wired and ready to go.

"Okay," Eddie said, standing back and taking one last look, "We double-checked everything. Let's go tell John we're ready."

Outside, John and Sheb had already moved the vehicles into a line and pointed them down the street.

"It's ready," Eddie told John as he approached.

John said, "Okay. Let's start all the vehicles, make sure they're running. Everybody load up except Eddie. Eddie will start the fuse; after he comes out of the mosque and gets in the vehicle, we will drive three hundred meters down the street to an empty lot on the right. I'll send the Iraqis down there now so we don't have to worry about them."

John had the Iraqis moving within a minute and gave Eddie the nod to go light the fuse. The other three team members waited patiently in the vehicles while Eddie went into the mosque. He was inside for only a matter of seconds, and as he came back outside, he strolled up to the vehicles with the casual confidence of someone who knows he got it right. Eddie said with total calm, "Let's go. The fire is lit."

The team rolled the three hundred meters to the designated spot and pulled up alongside the waiting Iraqis. Everyone got out of the vehicles to get a better look at the upcoming show.

Eddie was keeping time. "One minute."

John anxiously waited to see how close Eddie's calculations would be. He had seen demo guys be off by as much as thirty seconds in the past.

Looking at his watch, Eddie started the countdown. "Ten, nine, eight, seven, six, five."

John wondered if the mosque would still be standing, if they had enough explosives to do the job. There was no point worrying too much about that, though, since he could always call in an aircraft to finish the job.

"Four, three, two." No matter how many times Eddie had been involved in demo operations, he was never prepared for the suddenness and the shock of an explosion. This one was no exception. On the count of two, the whole team felt a rush of air against their faces and the vibration of the ground as the mosque exploded. The minaret dropped about ten feet, then slowly tilted and collapsed over the top of the dome. The whole team, even the Iraqis, were smiling and cheering. Everyone turned to congratulate Eddie.

But Eddie wasn't smiling at all. He shook his head. "Off by two seconds."

John laughed and said, "Let's go check it out."

The team pulled up to a pile of rubble. Only a small, six-foot-high section of the dome wall was still standing. Eddie immediately started to walk in and around the rubble, taking notes.

John turned to Sheb. "Now there's a pretty mosque."

"Amen," Sheb agreed.

John wasn't one to waste time. Exiting the vehicle he barked orders. "Call the marine commander and give him an update, and then get the PSC-5 up so we can send a sit-rep back to Baghdad."

Miguel joined John on the street, and both of them stared at the rubble for several minutes without saying anything. Finally Miguel looked at John and said, "For a minute there I thought we didn't have enough explosives to do the job. That's the last time I question Eddie's expertise."

John didn't look at Miguel, but said, "Eddie knows what he's doing, but more importantly, he loves what he does."

Sheb yelled for John. "I have the marine commander on the radio, and he said that we are to stand fast because the entire force has been ordered to stop the assault."

"Why would they stop it?" Miguel asked.

"I don't know, but I'll find out," John replied.

As John and Miguel approached Sheb, three Hummers came up the street from the west to meet them. They pulled up beside John, and a marine lieutenant jumped out.

"Sergeant Smith, we have been told to hold up. They are going to try and negotiate."

"Negotiate with who?" John asked, confused.

The lieutenant went on to explain that the mayor of Fallujah had called the Iraqi interim government and asked them to do something because there were bodies lying everywhere. The Iraqi government then told the U.S. military commanders to cease-fire so they could attempt to negotiate with the terrorists.

"Negotiate with a terrorist!" John said, shaking his head.

The lieutenant said, "That's what I was told."

John thanked the lieutenant and then watched him leave the area. Miguel came over and asked, "What's going on?"

"Go get Eddie and meet me and Sheb at the Toyota."

John explained the situation once everyone was gathered around the truck. Just as he expected, their reaction was like his. Even the less experienced Miguel said, "That shit ain't gonna work."

He was right! John knew that trying to negotiate with a terrorist was a waste of breath. He compared this with trying to reason with an obnoxious drunk in a bar—they simply would not listen. John also knew that calling these negotiations was a favorite tactic used by the terrorists to slow the momentum of the advancing Americans, and in the end, America would have to go in and clear the town anyway. The difference was, the terrorists would have fortified their positions, so the next time the operations would cost more lives.

"John we're getting a message on the PSC-5 from Baghdad," Sheb said.

John expected it to be the same message they had just received from the marines, but he wasn't prepared for what came over the data net. Sheb watched John send and receive messages for the next ten minutes. Everyone could tell that this was not good news just by watching John's expressions.

When John finished with the radio, he said to everyone, "They want us to take the commandos back to Baghdad."

John held up his hand before anybody could say anything. "Let me finish. Command feels that bringing the commandos back now, including the quitters, would be a great PR move, great for the media. They're also concerned that if we stay out here long enough, there won't be a commando unit left—all will have quit." John continued, "They want to bring all commandos from all units back and consolidate them at one location to salvage what's left."

Sheb was the first to speak up. "So where does that leave us?"

John replied, "We will go back and reconsolidate with the rest of our team at the house in south Baghdad, then fall in on the mission they are doing."

Eddie said, "When do we do all this?"

"This afternoon. Since there is a cease-fire, Command feels that now is the best time."

John added, "Miguel, do you have anything to say?"

"No," replied Miguel simply.

"If nobody has anything more to say …" John paused for a moment before continuing. "This is what we need to do. Sheb, call the marines and let them know it's been fun but we got to go. Then call Command and let them know we should be back in Baghdad at about 1700 this afternoon. Eddie and Miguel, round up all the quitters and get them ready to roll as soon as we get back to the marine compound."

"I'll brief Nadeem and the rest of the Iraqis that are with us on the plan. We roll in fifteen minutes." John knew the guys were taking this hard; it would undoubtedly seem to them that they had been fighting for nothing. He also expected Nadeem and his bunch of loyal commandos to be pissed, especially about letting the quitters return to Baghdad with them.

"Hey guys," John said, looking at Eddie, Miguel, and Sheb. "You did a fantastic job out here. Let's stay focused so we can do another fantastic job when we get to Baghdad."

The teammates nodded.

PART II
Blackmail

Conduct a thorough analysis of your knowledge, skills, and abilities; only then will you know if you're right for the job.

—*Unknown*

1

The team drove through the streets of southern Baghdad for the first time in over a week. Not enough time for any significant changes, but John did notice that more people appeared to be working, more shops were open, and quite a few vendors were selling fruit and vegetables from the backs of trucks or out of small wagons along the main roads. This has to be a good thing; if the people were working, they were not fighting.

The teammates had said their good-byes to the Iraqi commandos over an hour ago. During the good-byes, everyone had promised they would stay in touch. John would miss Nadeem, but knew he would never see him again.

This happened all the time, especially in John's unit. They would work with an individual for a couple of years, party with him, go fishing with him, and help him with home improvement projects. The team would develop a strong bond that they thought was unbreakable, but then an amazing thing would happen. One of the members would get assigned to a different team, abruptly putting an end to the friendship. They could no longer hang out together, even though they still called each other "friends." Some people occasionally made feeble attempts at maintaining some type of relationship with a parted buddy, but the effort was inevitably wasted, and the so-called friendship would disappear.

So the Americans had parted ways with Nadeem and the remaining commandos and would now be stationed at a base in northern Baghdad. Their training was to resume at this base; another Special Forces team had the honor of conducting that training.

"See the smoke stacks?" Eddie asked John as they motored toward their base.

"Yes," John said, simply.

The smoke stacks Eddie was referring to rose on the skyline of south Baghdad and were distinguishable from miles away. They were belching massive amounts of smoke—another good sign. It meant that the oil refinery was operating. It was not working at full capacity, but at least it was working. Watching the crap that poured out of the stacks, John had to laugh.

"What's so funny?" Eddie said as he swerved around an abandoned vehicle.

"I wonder what the American EPA would say about the shit coming out of the smoke stacks."

Eddie sneered slightly. "Who cares what the EPA would say? We have to breathe that shit every day. The team house is right beside it."

John didn't answer as they turned onto a section of road they used to call RPG alley. There had been more attacks by rocket-propelled grenades on this stretch of road than any other place in Baghdad. As they drove off the overpass, John could see the American military vehicles parked up and down the road at one-hundred-meter intervals. He also noticed that an Iraqi policeman manned every intersection of the road. This, John thought, should be a good deterrent against attacks.

John's attention again drifted back to the smoke stacks as they came closer to the oil refinery. Eddie was right about having to breathe that junk. He wondered if someone would ever test it to determine the amount of toxins that were pouring into the atmosphere.

Eddie slowed the Toyota down and made the final turn into the oil refinery compound. John could see the checkpoint.

He could live with the toxic fumes because to get to their team house, they had to pass two oil refinery checkpoints and then pass through their own military checkpoint, all of which were manned by Iraqis. He knew the only other area in Baghdad that was more secure was the Green Zone—the hub of the United States and Coalition Headquarters, located in central Baghdad.

The Americans took their time going through the refinery checkpoints. John wanted to make sure all the guards could see his face, so they would get used to him. He also took the time to make small talk with the guards. Rapport-building was the key to success when dealing with the Iraqis. The Iraqis especially liked when an American went out of his way to try and speak their language.

John's language ability was the best on the team and this very important quality had bailed the team out of some sticky situations. Although his base language was the Egyptian dialect, the Iraqis understood what he had to say. Having the Egyptian dialect was, in itself, a conversational piece. Many Iraqis had said to him, "*Tatkalim Masri?*" (You speak Egyptian?). Some had even turned up their noses at John's Egyptian dialect, asking, "Why do you speak Egyptian?"

John understood this sort of resentment, which he had experienced in Jordan, Saudi Arabia, and other Middle Eastern countries. He suspected that each person thought that their own dialect was the only proper way to speak the Arabic language. Still, his ability to speak the language at all had gone a long way toward establishing rapport with the natives.

John used another technique to establish good relations with the Iraqis. He would tell them that he was married and had five children—four boys and one girl. When John told this lie, whomever he was talking to would look at him with a newfound respect. The family was the most important thing in an Iraqi's life next to Allah, and the more children one had, the better—especially sons.

So John and Eddie shook hands with several of the guards and exchanged pleasantries to build relationships. Eddie was also getting very good at "meet and greets," and like John, he had picked up a lot of the Iraqi dialect.

It took them twenty minutes to get through both of the oil refinery checkpoints, with all the talking and handshakes. John knew that it would take at least that long to get through their military checkpoint. The team had hired sixteen Iraqis to guard their compound. As another benefit for the team, most of the guards lived within a mile of the team house. The level of trust was much higher when one's Iraqi employees lived in the same area as they worked. Nobody wanted to cause problems in their own back yard. Why would they? They were paid well, provided with medical treatment for them and their families, and they were given other amenities as well, such as air conditioners for their homes.

John recognized Omar as he approached the vehicle, and sent his friend a greeting. *"Ahlan, sadeeky."*

They spent the next twenty minutes reintroducing themselves to the guard force.

The captain, who had watched their approach from the second floor balcony, walked out to the front gate to personally greet the arrivals. He thought to himself, it will be good to have the whole team back together again.

For the last three months, the Special Forces team had been carrying out a split mission. John had taken four members of the team—Eddie, Sheb, Miguel, and Larry—and trained, fought, and lived with a company of Iraqi commandos. Meanwhile, Captain Rinehart and the remaining four members of the team had been conducting intelligence collection.

This mission was hard for the captain; with only five personnel including him, the team was spread very thin because of a rule put out by Command. The rule was that whenever the team needed to meet an intelligence source to get information from him, they would be required to take two vehicles and four people. Any time a member of the team went anywhere, there must be two vehicles with at least two personnel per vehicle. The captain understood the thought process behind this. It was a security issue, and it was a good rule, but with only five guys total, he would have a problem when two meetings were scheduled at or near the same time. There simply weren't enough men to meet both sources and obey the rule.

Needless to say, the captain had let his men break the rule on more than one occasion. Things were already a little better ever since John had sent Larry back from Fallujah, and the whole team being back together again took a lot of pressure off everyone.

Secretly he was extremely glad John was returning for another reason; there had been a personality conflict going on at the team house since day one. Jeff the senior weapons officer and Mike the senior medic had been at each other's throats since the team had been formed.

Jeff tried to act like he was the team sergeant. Although he had only three years of experience in Special Forces, he thought he was an expert in everything. This was Mike's first combat tour, and Jeff—who had already had a six-month tour in Iraq plus a tour in Afghanistan—was constantly using his combat experience to belittle Mike.

Jeff and Mike were the same rank and they both had the same amount of seniority. Nevertheless, the captain knew that Mike had reached the end of his patience with Jeff, and something was going to blow eventually.

The captain knew this was a common problem among Special Forces soldiers. There was constant bragging: "I've been on more deployments than you have." "I have more experience than you." "I've been to more schools than you."

That was one of the many things the captain liked about John. He never cared about what you'd done; he only cared about what you were doing or what you could do.

But this feud wasn't even the captain's biggest concern; he was more worried about junior communications sergeant Bruce and Wally, the team's junior engineer. Both were young and impressionable, and Jeff was having an enormous impact on their behavior. The captain was afraid that they were starting to look up to Jeff as a role model, which he considered to be far from a good thing. The last thing the captain wanted was a team full of braggarts and people who disrespected their equals.

The captain had to be truthful with himself; he was having a hard time dealing with this. He was glad for John's return.

He decided not to tell John about the personality conflict for a couple of days. He knew that Jeff and Mike would go at each other soon, and John was sure to hear about their dispute or see it firsthand. The captain would explain the whole situation once John had been exposed to the problem. He didn't have to wait long.

2

John was totally focused on his steak. It was the first decent meal he'd had in a couple of weeks, and he wanted to savor every bite of it. He tried to take his time and even made a conscious effort to eat slowly, but it wasn't working. The steak tasted too good!

Discovering the little comforts that a person took for granted while living in the United States never ceased to amaze him, like the availability of this delicious meal. He made a mental note to himself, "Make sure you kiss the ground when you get back to the United States."

The dinner table was buzzing with conversation; everyone was swapping stories. He could tell by the tone of the conversation that the Baghdad boys were a little jealous of the Fallujah fighters, but secretly he was pleased at the jealousy, which meant that the guys who had had to remain behind in Baghdad wanted to go and fight. It was always better to have people that wanted to fight as opposed to guys that sat around and waited for someone else to get the job done.

The men enjoyed a nonstop flow of conversation and stories since sitting down for supper together. John figured that this was the best way to get caught up on each other's missions. With his steak finished, John leaned back in his chair and listened more closely to some of the stories; he laughed at some and commented on others.

Miguel told the story about Sheb being shot in the body armor and having the breath knocked out of him, then how John had messed with him about it when he had first come to inside the mosque. This brought laughter from everyone including Sheb, who proudly stood up, lifted up his shirt, and paraded around the table showing off his bruise.

Bruce told a story of how they raided a car dealership that had been suspected of financing the insurgency through the sales of civilian vehicles. The Americans just happened to be the dealership's best customers. The irony of the story brought another round of laughter from the team.

Mike jumped in, telling a story about the time when the Baghdad boys had sat on a roof all night watching a section of road that was known for ambushing American convoys. During the vigil, three guys had attempted to emplace an improvised explosive device, but the team opened fire and killed all of them before they could set the IED.

Mike was unable to finish the story, though, because Jeff interrupted him. "You didn't shoot anybody. I was the one who shot everyone."

The dinner table instantly got quiet.

Mike responded to Jeff's comment sarcastically with, "Oh, I'm sure. The three other people probably shouldn't have even taken a shot, since you were there to shoot everybody. Maybe we should have sent you out by yourself, since you killed everyone single-handedly."

Jeff grunted and said, "We'll talk about this later."

But Mike would have none of it. "Why don't we talk about this now?"

"This is where I talk and you listen!" Jeff yelled, his face glowing red now.

John looked over at the captain after this last exchange and raised his eyebrows. Captain Rinehart just mouthed the word, "Later."

Members of the team already had started to leave the table after the outburst. Not much laughing and kidding going on now, John observed. It only took one asshole shooting off his mouth with negativities to change the attitude of the entire team.

After everyone had left the table the captain sat down with John and explained what was going on.

"Sir, why haven't you told Jeff to stop harassing Mike?" John asked.

The captain replied, "I tried to talk to him about it, and after our talks the situation would die down for a few days. But then they would be right back at it; Jeff feels he has to explain every detail of every day and every event to Mike."

John leaned his head back and exhaled deeply. He thought to himself how he didn't need this. It was just kids squabbling, that's all. Things were so much easier out in Fallujah, John thought, where you could just drive around and kill bad guys. Now it was time to play daddy.

The captain awaited John's opinion. "I'll talk to both of them tonight," John said. He called to Mike as he was passing by the dining room that moment.

"Do you want me to stay?" Captain Rinehart asked.

"No, sir. Let me try my way first, and if that don't work, we'll both sit down with them and try to clear this up." The captain nodded and took off as Mike approached.

Mike sat right down, and John decided to waste no time. "What's going on between you and Jeff?"

For the next thirty minutes John listened patiently as Mike talked about the bickering between him and Jeff. When Mike was finished John said, "Do you remember when I told you guys about long deployments, how living close together for so long you tend to get on each other's nerves? Little things start to irritate you that months ago you wouldn't have even thought about. For instance, a guy may leave his dirty clothes lying on the floor instead of putting them in a laundry bag. He may have been doing this the entire time you've been here, but it only starts to bother you now."

Mike nodded. John enjoyed talking to Mike because he was such an attentive listener. When Mike finally spoke it was to the point. "So what am I supposed to do about Jeff?"

John smiled because he knew that this was the easy part of this whole situation. Jeff, on the other hand, would be another story.

"Okay, Mike," John began. "This is what you're going to do. Avoid Jeff when possible. Do not engage in conversation around him unless it's absolutely necessary. If he says anything demeaning to you, let me know immediately. Remember, you work for me, so if Jeff tells you to do anything, tell him to come and talk with me. Any questions?"

Mike started standing up to go. "No questions, Sergeant. I'll try it, but I really don't know how much more of this I can take. Sometimes I feel like kicking his ass will be the only way to get through his thick skull."

"Just be patient, and don't kick his ass—not yet anyway. There may come a time when I might whip his ass with you, but for right now, let me try and talk with him. Remember, you work for *me*. Tell Jeff to come down here so I can talk with him."

When Jeff arrived a few minutes later, he took a seat in front of John and immediately started talking. "I know what this is about. Mike's been complaining about me; he's a turd and he's stupid."

John said, "Tell me what he's done that's so bad."

"Wally and him wanted money from the operations fund to build an additional fighting position in the northwest corner of the compound," Jeff said.

"What's wrong with that?"

"He's not in charge here and doesn't have enough experience to make decisions like that." Jeff wanted to continue, but John held up his hand and told him to stop.

"First thing, Jeff, when it comes to Force Protection and security, money should never be an issue no matter whose idea it is. Second, the way you talk to Mike is unacceptable. In fact, speaking that way to anyone is rude and unprofessional."

John tried to continue but Jeff cut him off. "I'm the best soldier on this team; I'm the only one that has produced any actionable intelligence. If it wasn't for me this team would fall apart!"

John lost all his patience. "You need to shut up! Now is when I talk and you listen!" Looking Jeff right in the eye, John continued. "You are not in charge. I am. Is that understood?"

Even though Jeff was boiling mad, he could not maintain eye contact with John. It was those fucking weird eyes of his. Jeff shifted his gaze and replied with a simple "Yes."

"Mike is the senior medic on this team, which means he answers to me and only me. Is that understood?"

Again Jeff answered with only a "Yes."

"We are here to fight terrorists. The last thing we need is the team imploding, so leave Mike alone! Is that understood?"

"Yes. Are we done Sergeant?" Jeff stood up, making to leave.

"No! Sit your ass down." John waited until Jeff was seated before continuing. "What else has he done that is so bad?"

Jeff was glad to have another chance to talk. "He had an electrician hook up the house to the local power grid. The power goes out about six hours every day and then we have to go out and fire up the generator until the power comes back on."

"What were you doing before this?"

"We ran the generator all the time and never had a break in power."

Trying to be patient and nice, John said, "To me, that sounds like a good thing. Being hooked up to local power should allow us to save the generator and make it last longer."

Jeff replied, "But the air conditioner doesn't get as cold when we're on local power, and when the power goes out it gets miserably hot by time the generator is up and running."

"The air conditioning?" John said incredulously as he fought hard not to break into laughter.

"Yes, I think we should leave the generator running full-time."

"And what if the generator goes tits up? How long will the air conditioning be out before we can get a replacement generator?" John couldn't hold the laughter back much longer.

Jeff was visibly irate. "Are we done, Sergeant?"

"We're done." John replied, unable to control his laughter.

After Jeff stormed out of the room, John leaned back in his chair and thought to himself, "Welcome back."

John remembered eleven years ago when he was in Somalia. Seven months living in a shit hole. No air conditioning. Everyone was extremely grateful on rare occasions when they managed to scrap together a couple of fans. The old saying was true: no matter what, soldiers will bitch about something, and they are never satisfied.

It all starts like this. In the beginning, you live out of your rucksack, sleep on the ground, and drink warm, brackish water. If you're lucky you brought enough socks to change them once a week. You start getting weary of sleeping out in the elements. The wind is not so bad, but when it rains you get miserable. Soon the sand has found its way into everything. At this point the only thing you're thinking about is how nice it would be to have a roof over your head.

As time goes on, you establish yourself at a base somewhere. This could be anything from an abandoned building to an army tent. Now that you have a roof over your head, you tend to forget about how bad it was sleeping out in the wind, sun, rain, and dust. So, are you thankful there's a roof over your head?

No!

Now you start complaining again because there are no lights in the building you're occupying, and you're tired of doing everything with a flashlight. Somehow someone on the team procures a generator, and now there's light!

Next you're lying on the ground inside your shelter trying to go to sleep, but you can't because the generator is too loud, and the last person to bed forgot to switch off the lights. The generator has to run all night because the team has hooked up its radio system to it, to save the Lithium batteries that would otherwise be used for the radios. But at least someone could turn out the lights. Instead of getting up and turning the lights off, you throw your poncho liner over your head to keep the light out of your eyes. In your mind you start thinking about the bed at home, how soft and comfortable it is.

Guess what? A few days pass and a support unit delivers army cots to your group. Now it's not so bad to get up and turn the lights off or go to the bathroom. Before when early morning came and you felt that discomfort of the morning piss coming on, you would continue to lie there tossing and turning in the hopes that the urge to take a leak would go away. Which is stupid because it won't go away, and it's too much effort to stand up, walk outside, and take a leak. But now that you have a cot, it makes life a lot easier. Instead of having to stand up, you can just roll off the side. Life is good. If only you had some cool water to drink, things would be perfect.

Once again the support unit comes through and delivers a refrigerator. Everyone is ecstatic and lends a hand packing it full of the bottled water that the support unit was also kind enough to deliver. Cold water! After drinking warm water for weeks the taste and feel of cold water running down your throat is pure ecstasy. Now you are one hundred percent satisfied. Still though, you're getting a little sick of eating those prepackaged MREs.

But the engineer on the team saves the day; he has contracted a local restaurant owner to supply meals. Twenty meals a day at one hundred dollars a week, delivered! The meals are a mix of beef, chicken, and goat. Each plate of food comes with rice and some raw vegetables. It tastes so good you swear that a five-star restaurant in the United States has personally catered your food.

What could you possibly bitch about now? You now have a roof over your head, lights, cold water, and a diverse diet. So what could possibly be the problem now?

Because you're eating local food, your stomach does a little hiccup in the middle of the night. It wakes you up! It's time to race as fast as you can to the bathroom trench that everyone uses to do his business. You start off running, but barely get out of the building before you realize that if you continue to run you'll crap your pants. The shit pit is a hundred meters away, but it looks like a thousand. You've now slowed down to a walk, holding you're stomach.

Must have been the tomatoes!

Halfway there you try to think about something else, but you feel the push coming on. It's time for the last resort; you clamp you butt cheeks together in an attempt to delay the inevitable. It works! Somewhat. Only twenty-five meters left, and you think you're going to make it! Your pace has slowed because you're no longer walking, but waddling like a duck, squeezing with all your effort. At twenty meters, you start unbuckling your pants! At fifteen meters, you think, "I can't crap in these pants because my other uniform is even dirtier."

Ten meters left, and your pants are now down below your ass cheeks. The end looks so near, but your ass cheeks are getting tired. Five meters; you're cussing the local food that days earlier you were praising.

You spin around and walk backwards the last meter as the volcano starts, most of it landing in the trench. As you're squatting over the trench the sense of relief is overwhelming. You're beaming with pride for having the discipline and strength to make it all the way, until you realize that you had forgotten to bring any toilet paper.

You glance to your left, then to your right, and you see one of your teammates through the dark at the other end of the pit in the same position as you find yourself.

Conversation starts, "Barely made it, Huh?"

"Yep, but I forgot the ass wipe."

"I got some."

"Nice night."

"Not bad."

You spend the next three days running to the shit pit every thirty minutes, drinking as much water as possible to counter the dehydration caused by the diarrhea, and swearing an oath that you'll never eat local food again.

At night you lay on your cot and sweat; partly from the heat, but mostly from the diarrhea. You toss and turn, and now you think to yourself, sure would be nice if we had *an air conditioner.*

John sat at the dining room table by himself, reminiscing, still laughing about Jeff's reliance on the precious air conditioning. He had crapped his pants on more than one deployment; can't do anything about it but laugh, he thought.

He went back to thinking about the team and tried to evaluate their current status. The team had a total of ten people. Larry was unreliable in a firefight, which he proved on the streets of Karmah.

Then there were Jeff and Mike, who were about to kill each other. Jeff was a hothead, but worst of all, he wasn't a team player.

If he fired Larry and Jeff, could the team continue the mission with only eight men? Should he wait and give them the chance to turn things around?

John decided to see how things played out over the next few days.

3

It was a lazy morning, the kind where the most active thing a person felt like doing was sitting in a comfortable chair and watching the sunrise.

John and the captain sat drinking coffee on the front porch of the house. One of the interpreters the team employed was spraying off the sidewalk with a water hose. Two mangy dogs that someone on the team had adopted were wrestling with each other in the grass.

John looked around the compound. It was a good place to have a base of operations.

An eight-foot wall topped with razor wire surrounded all the main buildings of the compound, which took the shape of a rectangle one hundred meters long and seventy meters wide. The only two ways to enter the compound consisted of two large, steel gates at opposite ends of the compound. The Iraqi guard force employed by the team guarded the first of these twenty-four hours a day, while the other gate was left unguarded. However, for anyone to approach the unguarded gate, they would have to drive on a small path that ran parallel to the outer wall, and entry to this path was also covered by the Iraqi guards, so it was completely secure.

The entirety of the compound's backside wall was on the water's edge of the Tigris River. It was a possibility, however remote, that someone could enter unauthorized from that direction, but they would still have to scale the wall and defeat the razor wire.

The compound consisted of three large buildings and one other small structure within those eight-foot walls. The biggest building was the team house itself. "House" was a loose term; it was more like a palace. At three stories high and with twenty-five different rooms, it could have easily housed thirty people or more.

The pool building lay beside the house, it was ninety feet long by forty feet wide. The pool itself was sixty feet by twenty feet and had an attached whirlpool. This building also acted as the laundry room. With two washers and two dryers, it was more than adequate for the team.

The last of the large buildings was the gym, which contained seven different cardio machines and two complete sets of free weights.

The fourth building was a small concrete structure that the team used as an arms room where they kept all the weapons they had confiscated over the last three months locked up. It had a solid foot of concrete for the ceiling, so there was no worry of a mortar busting through and igniting their stockpile.

Outside the compound wall, a local farmer's fields bordered two sides of the compound, stretching out from the wall for a distance of two hundred meters. The final side not bordering the river was surrounded by the team's guard force housing area.

Yep, John thought as he rose to get some more coffee, this is a damn good place. Come to think of it, he couldn't remember living at a nicer place while being overseas. He sat back down with the captain after refilling his coffee and took another look around. How could anyone bitch or complain about a setup like this? he thought, remembering the previous night's discussion with Jeff.

"Anybody else out of bed?" The captain asked him.

"Nah."

Nobody was out of bed yet because it was only five in the morning. John and the captain continued talking, the captain was updating him on the overall situation in their whole coverage area, and their area was huge! It encompassed the entire region of south Baghdad, from the Tigris River to the city of Hillah—over fifty miles.

The captain filled John in about the local sheiks and what influence they had on the insurgency. He brought up the fact that they might be able to build rapport with these local leaders and use their influence to quell some of the violence.

The captain was continuing to talk about the sheiks when John heard a light thumping noise in the distance. He turned to the captain and interrupted him, saying, "I just heard something that sounded awful familiar; I think we are about to be …"

A mortar exploded!

The mortar landed outside the compound, cutting off John mid-sentence. The explosion was about fifty meters outside the wall, in the farmer's field. A few seconds later another mortar exploded, but this one was even farther away from the compound wall.

John took a sip of coffee and looked toward the captain to tell him that whoever was shooting mortars at them wasn't very effective and needed some more training, but the captain was already through the door to the inside. He had even abandoned his coffee cup. John just continued to sip his coffee, waiting to see if there were any more mortars. He could hear people stirring inside the house now and thought, nothing like a few explosions to get everybody out of bed—can't hit the snooze button on an alarm like that.

No more mortars came in, so John took the opportunity to top off his coffee. It was nice just to get up in the morning, sit on the front porch, and have a few cups. These were the little things that he had missed. But with mortars exploding all the time, John, for the first time in his military career, thought about retirement. It had never occurred to him before, but he was only two years from minimum requirement of twenty years of service. He was comforted by the thought that in a couple years he could sit on his own porch and drink coffee without being interrupted by someone trying to kill him with a mortar attack.

As he walked back inside to fill up one more time, Sheb stuck his head out of the bathroom and said, "What's up?"

"Just a couple of mortars, nothing to worry about."

Sheb closed the bathroom door and mumbled something. John thought it sounded like, "How can they be so rude as to disturb someone when they're taking a shit."

Several other members of the team were milling about; a few even had all their combat gear on. John looked on with interest, then walked back outside and resumed his place on the porch. The guys who had spent the last ten days fighting in Fallujah were used to mortars and explosions. John was simply amazed at what a person could grow accustomed to.

Within five minutes, the captain reappeared through the front door dressed in full battle gear. John looked over the top of his coffee cup and said, "Where you off to, sir?"

"Getting ready in case we're attacked," He said nervously.

"Sir, I'm positive it's only harassment fire," John said. Then he added, "Does this happen often?"

"About three times a week."

"Any damage?"

"They bounced one off the top of the gym, but it didn't do any damage."

"How long has this been happening?"

"For the last three weeks."

John paused for a moment to think as several other members began to filter out of the house. Sheb, dressed in shorts and flip-flops, said through a big yawn, "I'm going back to bed."

Bruce came out in full battle gear also, but when he saw John relaxing in a chair with a cup of coffee, barefoot and dressed only in shorts, he immediately turned around and went back inside.

John motioned for the captain to sit down. "Sir, it's obvious that whoever is mortaring us knows were here and knows were American. What have you guys done to try and counter this?"

"We have been trying to gather intelligence on them through our sources, but nothing has turned up yet. One of the Iraqi guards, Omar, says he might know who is doing it, but even if he's right there's not much we can do about it. Omar also says he thinks they are being paid by someone to mortar us."

"How much do we trust Omar?" John asked.

"As much as any of them. He has stuck by us through everything."

John sat back in his chair and thought for several minutes as the captain watched him with interest. He had not worked with John in a combat scenario because of the split mission, but he'd heard stories of John's previous combat tours. But this would be the first time he would actually get to work hand-in-hand with the combat veteran.

He noticed John starting to smile, so he asked him, "What are you smiling at, John?"

"Sir, I think I'll get another cup of coffee and stroll down to the gate and wait for Omar to come to work. If I understand the shift change right, he should be coming to work in thirty minutes or so, is that right?" The captain nodded and looked as if he was going to say something, but John went inside in pursuit of more coffee.

With no reason to stay on the patio, the captain also went inside the house. He started to feel a little silly about getting spun up over a couple of mortars as he started to take off his combat gear, but you never knew.

He was replayed his conversation with John, wondering if John had somehow found a way to deal with the mortar attacks. Maybe there was something that he overlooked? John had a reputation of looking at things differently, the captain knew, but he did not see any way of catching the guys that were firing the mortars, except by blind luck.

4

John spent two hours talking with Omar then returned to the house and went in search of Jeff. Upon the team's being stationed in Iraq, Jeff had been assigned as the sergeant accountable for the team's operations fund, on-hand cash issued to a team to help them operate independently. "Jeff, I need one thousand dollars from the operations fund, right now."

Startled, Jeff responded, "What for?"

John didn't want to argue with him again so he took the hard-ass approach. "Because I said so! You'll have a receipt or accountability by tomorrow morning."

Jeff, grumbled to himself, went to the team safe and retrieved the money. John took the cash and counted it out in front of Jeff; afterwards both men were satisfied that it was a thousand dollars. John stuck the money into the pocket of his shorts, and left the house again, heading down to the main gate.

The captain watched all this with growing interest. John had only been back one day and he already had Jeff listening to him. The captain started to think that the tension within the team might be quelled after all.

The shining glint in John's eyes the captain saw when John returned to the house after spending another hour talking with Omar told him that something good had just happened. John approached. "Sir, we need to talk about something."

They went to the operations room and closed the door. For the next hour they discussed what John had learned. Afterwards, John stuck his head out of the operations room door looking for anybody. Spotting Wally cleaning his gun while watching a movie, John said, "Wally, go tell everyone we have a meeting in thirty minutes."

The entire team had assembled in the briefing room by the time the captain and John emerged from their private meeting a couple minutes later. John looked around and noticing that everyone was present, he began. "Tonight we are going to try and ambush the guys who are mortaring us. We will take one of the civilian vans to transport six of us to conduct the ambush."

Before John could continue, Jeff chimed in. "We're not taking a Hummer?"

John answered, "No."

Jeff continued immediately. "We need to take at least two vehicles and one needs to be a Hummer."

John hung his head, but to humor Jeff he asked, "Why must we take two?"

"It's a security issue. I'm not going anywhere without a Hummer."

John smiled. "Good, then you can stay here and watch the radios. Now don't interrupt again; if anyone has any questions, wait till I'm finished."

John continued with the brief. "The following six people will be going: Captain Rinehart, Sheb, Miguel, Eddie, Mike, and myself. The rest of you will remain here. Bruce, make sure the radio is set up properly for Jeff. After that, Bruce, man the Hummer with Wally and Larry so you're ready to go in case we need you. Jeff, like I said before you will monitor the radio."

John explained the details. "The six members that I mentioned will leave the team house at 2100 and will travel one and half kilometers along the river going south. Once we reach this location," John pointed a map of the city, "we leave the van with two people inside, the captain and Eddie. The four remaining team members will travel on foot along the canal that flows inland and set up on the large four-way intersection, here." Once again John pointed at the map, then gave everyone ample time to look at the location before continuing.

"Once the team of four reaches the intersection, they will hide in the ditch and wait for the bad guys to show up with the mortars. Two people will hide on each side. It will be Sheb and Mike on one side and Miguel and I on the other."

"If the bad guys show up, I will give the signal to close in on the enemy. When we come out of our hiding places, we will move toward the enemy, nice and slow, trying to get as close as possible before opening fire. I'll initiate the attack by opening fire first. As soon as the firing starts the captain and Eddie will drive the van to where we are and pick us up."

"Once all the bad guys are dead, Sheb and Mike will search their vehicle and start gathering all their weapons. Miguel, you and I will search the bodies. Eddie, when you get to our location, lend Sheb and Mike a hand loading all the weapons into our van. Captain Rinehart, Miguel and I will need your help to push their vehicle into the canal."

"If nobody shows up by midnight, we pack it up and return to base."

Before anyone could start with questions, John said, "Let's go outside and go through some rehearsals. I'll answer any questions outside while we practice."

Everyone left the room to get ready for rehearsals. The captain stopped John and said, "John, we have to do something about Jeff."

"I know," John replied, but left it at that. They went to join the team outside.

For the next two hours, the team rehearsed every aspect of the operation. John included every member in the rehearsals. As he told them, "You never know, someone could sprain their ankle during rehearsals, and I may have to swap positions around. I think it's better for everyone to know what's going on." This had always been John's philosophy.

After rehearsals, John told everybody to catch a little rest and that equipment check would be at 2030 hours.

Sheb passed John, laughing.

"Mind telling me what is so funny, Sheb?" John asked.

"Your equipment checks. You don't care what a person wears or carries as long as he has a gun and plenty of ammunition," Sheb said in good humor.

John laughed. "Fine, if you want to make fun of me, you can do the equipment check."

Sheb continued walking away, still chuckling, when Mike said, "John, do we need to bring any flex ties to secure detainees with?" Sheb put his arm around Mike and started walking with him toward the house. He knew he would have to explain to Mike that they were not going to detain anyone.

John had been told by a sergeant major one time, "If you're in a fight and a bad guy drops his weapon and throws his hands in the air to surrender, you will need to detain him, so every member of your team should be carrying flex ties."

John never answered or acknowledged this statement. His thought was, "If I'm in a fight and some bad guy drops his weapon with the intention of surrendering, I'm going to shoot him!" In John's mind, detaining the man would do nothing but aid the insurgency.

The team rolled out of the gate at exactly 2100 hours. Everyone looked bored. John realized that he had unwittingly brought everyone with him that had been in Fallujah, except Mike and the captain. He knew that he would have to change it up in the future, because taking the same people every time would in itself cause problems among the teammates.

The ten-minute van ride was uneventful, and so was the walk to the ambush point which also took only ten minutes. They set up in a good place for hiding; if the mortar crew showed up, they wouldn't have a clue that someone was lurking in the shadows waiting to kill them. John thought that that was a fitting end to someone who drove around shooting mortars. If a person was sitting on their porch drinking coffee when a mortar fell on them, they never had a chance to fight back. With this ambush, the tables were turned.

There was a big difference between what the team was about to do and what the terrorists were doing. The team was going to selectively kill, but when a terrorist fired a mortar into a compound he didn't care who he killed.

Thankfully, the wait wasn't long. Shortly after 2200 the four team members watched as car lights slowly approached from the south, headed right for them. Sheb thought that this had to be just someone out driving. The odds of them catching the mortar crew on the first night were impossibly low. Missions of this type usually took four to five attempts to catch someone in the act. Sheb knew that John was good at figuring out the enemy, but there was no way that he could have guessed it right on the first attempt, and on the first day since their return, to boot.

The car slowed as it passed them and then came to a stop right in the middle of the intersection. Sheb and Mike lay motionless, but Sheb was still thinking this was a random person out for a drive—then they heard the signal from John.

All four members stood up slowly and started to advance on the unsuspecting terrorists. Sheb knew that they would be able to get within twenty meters of the terrorists under cover of darkness before being spotted. The three guys were also distracted because they had to set up their mortar tube, allowing the team to get even closer undetected. Sheb couldn't believe they had caught them on the first try.

John and Miguel moved down the right side of the canal road, while Sheb and Mike advanced on the left. As they drew closer, Sheb noticed that two of the three terrorists were on his side. Sheb glanced over and noticed that John had his weapon against his cheek and was about to fire, when Mike jumped the gun and began shooting. In a flash the whole team was shooting and moving.

They kept up a steady rate of fire as they continued moving toward the terrorists. Only when they had reached the car did they stop shooting, because at that point anyone could tell that the three terrorists were dead.

John immediately started searching the bodies and Miguel said, "Here come the captain and Eddie. I guess they heard the firing."

John looked down the canal road to the west and recognized the van coming toward them. Miguel searched the other two terrorists as Sheb pulled mortar rounds out of the enemy's vehicle. Mike was just standing in one spot and staring at the bodies.

John snapped him out of it. "Mike! Help Sheb with the weapons."

Mike quickly sprang into action helping Sheb with the weapons and the rest of the vehicle search, but he was visibly shaken up by the brutality with which they had attacked. He had started the firing, but the other three members had continued to shoot until the bodies looked like Swiss cheese. Mike had engaged an enemy before this, but never at this close and personal a range and not with the viciousness displayed here. He could only hope John wasn't mad at him for firing early, but the adrenalin had gotten the best of him.

The rest of the search and the loading of the weapons took less than five minutes. As they pushed the terrorist's car into the canal, the captain said, "What about the bodies?"

John replied, "Leave them. The locals will find them and take care of all the arrangements. You know the culture; they can't stand when a body is uncovered and unattended to. Total strangers will find these bodies and make sure they are taken care of according to their customs."

John looked around and was satisfied that everything was taken care, and Sheb said, "All equipment accounted for."

"Okay, let's go."

Sheb looked out the window of the van as he climbed in and observed John talking to one of the dead men's bodies and placing a piece of paper on his chest. On the ride back to the team compound, Sheb never got a chance to ask John what he had done or what he had said because he was on the radio talking with Jeff, letting the rest of the team know that they were coming back to the compound after having killed the people who had been shooting the mortars.

The van pulled up beside the front door and Bruce and Wally met them with a barrage of questions.

"How did you know they would be at that spot?"

"How many did you kill?"

"What happened, what happened?"

John ignored all these questions and said, "Equipment inventory, take care of the van, AAR in thirty minutes."

By the time the whole team had assembled in the briefing room, John was already seated and taking excessive care in cleaning his weapon. He motioned for the captain to begin, and the captain spent the next thirty minutes explaining everything in detail..

That morning when John learned that the guard Omar might know something about the mortar attacks, he spent the next two hours talking to him. In the course of his talks, he learned that Omar had a cousin. This cousin's job was to find people and pay them to mortar the team's compound.

Omar's cousin had refused to do this at first; the last thing he wanted was to get involved in the war. But after his family was threatened, he felt there was no choice. The cousin said that the money was coming from an unknown source, and it was delivered to him by way of a young boy acting as a courier.

After talking with Omar it became obvious that the compound had never been mortared while he was there, at work. With that knowledge, it was plain to John that his cousin didn't want Omar hurt. It was also clear that the cousin was in control of the timing of the attacks.

John had taken a gamble; he gave Omar a thousand dollars to give to his cousin with instructions to pay the bad guys and make sure the compound got mortared. John worked out the details with Omar, making sure the attack would be that night.

The captain concluded the report. "While we were conducting the ambush, Omar moved his cousin's family into his own house. The cousin will also be staying there from this point on; and since Omar's house is only one hundred meters outside our compound, they should be relatively safe."

Jeff stood up, clearly mad. "Are you saying the thousand dollars I gave you out of the operations fund was used to pay terrorists to fire mortars into our own compound?"

John reached into his pocket, pulled out the thousand dollars, and threw it to Jeff. "Dead terrorists! I recovered the money from one of the bodies."

Jeff sat down with a disgruntled look on his face. "Yeah, and what if you wouldn't have recovered the money? Then what?"

John was getting angry with Jeff again. "I don't care about what might have happened! I only care about what did happen! Now hold off with your criticism and comments and let the captain finish."

The captain continued with the brief. "When John told me what he had in mind, I was a little skeptical at first, but after sitting down and hearing it all the way through it sounded just crazy enough to work. Since nothing else seemed to be working, I figured what the hell."

"We sat down this afternoon and planned everything out, including the location of the ambush. We knew they were shooting sixty-millimeter mortars at us, so they had to be setting up and firing at us from a fairly close location—we figured it was no more than two kilometers away. The angle at which the mortars were coming into the compound led us to deduce the general area from which they were firing. Studying the map, it was plain that they were using the canal road to get close enough to us. It was the most remote area, and using the big intersection where all the canal roads meet would allow them four different directions of escape. John also suggested this spot to Omar, and his cousin later confirmed that as the location they were indeed firing from. Now that we knew the time and the place, the rest was easy."

The captain looked over at John, "Do you want to add anything else?"

"I think that covers the general scheme of it. Who has questions?" John asked.

Mike was the first. "How in the hell did you get Command to approve this mission?"

The captain answered this one. "They don't know, and that's the way it will stay. Everyone in the room knows they would never approve something like this."

Sheb was the next to speak. "John, what did you leave on the body of that dead guy, and what could you possibly have to say to a dead man?" Nobody but Sheb had seen this exchange, so the rest of the team was extremely anxious to hear John's reply.

"I pinned a death card to the dead man's shirt, which said in Arabic, 'These men were killers of women and children, and God has sent them to hell.' After that I told him I hoped he was enjoying his virgins."

After a moment of silence, John also added, "Look, I know it was a gamble. Many things could have gone wrong, but the alternative was to sit on our asses and get mortared three times a week, and that is unacceptable."

Before anyone else could ask another question one of the house's cell phones started ringing. Sheb answered it, and the look on his face told John it was not good news.

Sheb handed the phone to John and said, "It's the company sergeant major, and he would like to speak with Sergeant Smith."

The captain looked at John and raised his eyebrows. John grabbed the phone and knew he was in trouble. The sergeant major never used John's last name when he addressed him.

John started to stare at Jeff as he sat down to talk with the sergeant major. The captain had never seen John make the expression that was on his face now. He could only describe the look as pure hatred, and it was all directed at Jeff.

Jeff could not handle the way John was staring at him, so he got up and left the room. The captain then told everyone to leave. He could tell by John's expressions that the sergeant major was chewing his ass. After ten minutes, John handed the phone to the captain. "The company commander would like to speak with you."

When the captain hung up the phone, he looked at John and asked, "How in the hell did they find out?"

"It's obvious that someone on the team told them, and I can guarantee you I know who did," John replied.

"Jeff?"

"Yes."

"We have to get rid of him," the captain said.

"Give me a little time to come up with something," John said as he stood up. "Right now I'm going to bed."

5

The captain had a hard time sleeping. He kept thinking about his talk with the commander. Actually it wasn't much of a talk; the commander basically just told him how much he was screwing up, and that he was on the verge of being replaced. The captain listened and took his ass-chewing; he understood the commander's concern, but the captain also knew that for them to get things done in a timely matter they would have to bend some of Command's rules.

The captain had tried to remind the commander of a slide given during their briefback, the in-depth outline covering the entire mission given to the Battalion commander several weeks before a Special Forces team deployment. This slide, called the contingency slide, told the commander of the need for timely action on "targets of opportunity." Captain Rinehart felt that if ever there was a target of opportunity, the terrorists mortaring their compound was it.

The Battalion commander receiving the briefback, back at Fort Campbell Kentucky, had seemed impressed with the enthusiasm of the team and had given his blessing concerning everything the team had briefed him about. So, to the captain that left only two possibilities: one, the commander had changed his mind and hadn't bothered to tell them; or two, he was getting pressure from higher up the chain of command. The captain figured it was the latter.

The thing that bothered him the most about last night's events was Jeff. The captain wasn't too concerned about the chain of command; what were they going to do? Fire him for killing some bad guys that were about to mortar his house? Not likely. Nah, the most disturbing thing was Jeff shooting off his mouth. What happens on a team stays on the team; this was an unwritten rule in Special Forces. He knew why Jeff had told Command about their operation—to get back at John.

Jeff was really inexperienced; everyone knew that the last person you wanted to piss off was John Smith. Relaxing in bed, thinking this over, the captain came to the conclusion that if John didn't fire Jeff soon, he would.

He rolled over and got up with the intent of waking John up so they could discuss the situation, but he found that John wasn't in his bed. Looking at his watch, the captain saw it was only 0430, but he smiled, knowing exactly where John would be.

As expected, John was sitting in the same chair as the day before, drinking coffee. The captain joined him.

"Don't you ever sleep?"

"Sir, the morning is the best part of the day. No point wasting it in bed, unless you have a woman with you. Plus, I needed to get some thinking done; can't do that while you're sleeping, either," John said.

"We need to talk about Jeff. We have to let him go, but I'm worried about him shooting off his mouth. You know as well as I do that Jeff is immature and a hothead. He will badmouth the team to anybody that will listen." The captain looked concerned.

John didn't say anything for a couple of minutes. He'd been thinking about this ever since he woke up. He remembered last fall when he had been assigned to the team. He had fired four team members in his first week as the team sergeant. He also started an intense training program that sparked renewed motivation in the remaining team members, including Jeff. John could even recall a conversation with the company sergeant major—Jeff had told the sergeant major that he thought ODA 451 was the best team around and was thankful that John Smith had taken charge.

The only reason John could think of that would turn Jeff's attitude around was that he didn't like being away from home. Jeff had been a good team player when they were back in the United States, but as soon as they had arrived in Iraq, his attitude had changed.

"So what are we gonna do about Jeff?" The captain asked once the silence got to him.

When John finally spoke the captain wasn't prepared for what came out of his mouth. "Sir, I think the boys have had a rough couple of weeks and should be allowed to relax. I think tonight we'll have a party in the pool house. Bring in some girls and break out the beer."

The captain didn't fully comprehend. "But what about Jeff?" The captain asked again.

"Don't worry, I have a plan. I'll fire him tomorrow, and I promise he won't say anything about what the team has done." He paused. "Is it okay for us to have a little party?" John added.

"Yes, but keep it down at the pool house. What is the plan with Jeff?" the captain asked once more.

But John stood up to get some more coffee. "You don't want to know."

Before he entered the house, he looked over his shoulder at the captain and said, "I know better than to ask this, but I have to. Do you want to participate in the party, sir?"

"No thanks."

John had known the captain wouldn't take part; he was one of the few married guys that actually didn't cheat on his wife. John had seen it for years—the minute guys left the United States they were looking to get a better deal than their wife. He guessed that when you wake up every morning and eat cornflakes for breakfast, it became almost impossible to turn down fruit loops when they were dangled in front of your face. John knew the nature of men. He himself had been married for six years, and although he never cheated on his wife, he still understood the temptation. Now he was counting on this temptation to protect the team.

John replenished his coffee and walked slowly toward the front gate, taking his time to enjoy the coolness of the morning. It was time to have a talk with another one of the guards.

This time it was Abdel. Abdel was a man who could get anything a person wanted—for the right price, of course. He wasn't a criminal or a terrorist, just a simple businessman trying to make a buck in a shattered economy.

Abdel was brewing tea on a small stove as John approached him with a greeting.

"*Sabaah il'xeer*, Abdel."

Always smiling, Abdel returned a greeting of his own, "*Sabaah il'noor*."

Abdel enjoyed talking with John; he was one of the few Americans who went out of his way to try and speak Arabic. Although John's Arabic was choppy and usually wrong grammatically, Abdel was just happy with the effort. But more importantly, he thought John truly understood their culture.

They talked for thirty minutes about nothing in general, when John finally asked Abdel if he could arrange for some girls to come by this evening. Abdel said this would be no problem, and asked how many girls he wanted. John told him that four should be enough, and then they haggled on the price, eventually settling on a price of three hundred dollars for all four girls for the entire night. John thought to himself, damn inflation, damn capitalism, just last year you could get the same thing for only one hundred dollars.

Knowing he could probably get some more selling done, Abdel added that he could get them some Viagra for only a dollar a pill. This sounded good to John, so he gave a hundred dollars to Abdel for the Viagra, and they both agreed that the three hundred for the girls would be paid that when they arrived. The girls would arrive at 2100 tonight, but the pills, Abdel said, could be delivered within the hour.

John walked away feeling satisfied that the guys would be taken care of tonight. He was also started thinking about how much he was starting to like this country. A person could have a good life here; on the outside looking in, the world looked at the religious aspect of the Muslim influence in Iraq and never had a clue what really went on. To John, this country was no different than the two dozen others he had visited. Money, sex, and power were what ruled here! Everyone had a price or a vice! It really wasn't bad here at all, except for the fact that you may be killed at any time. Of course, a person could just as easily get killed on the streets of almost any major city in the United States.

Now the only thing left to do was to ask all the guys on the team who wanted to take part in tonight's festivities. When John returned to the house he spotted Sheb heading for the toilet. "Sheb, tell everyone there will be a meeting at 0900."

"Everything all right, boss?" Sheb asked.

"Yes," John replied.

"Is it about last night's operation?"

"Some of it, but I have some information to put out also."

The team was assembled when John entered the briefing room at 0900. Some of them looked tired, while others just looked bored. John could understand the boredom; he hated meetings, too. Most of them accomplished nothing and were conducted mainly for the dissemination and sharing of information, but he knew this meeting would perk them up somewhat.

Before John could speak, Mike stood up and said, "Sorry about last night. I should have waited for the signal to fire."

John waved him off. "Don't worry about it. The goal was to kill everyone, and you did fine. In fact, everyone did a good job last night. Mike, remember what I always said before, 'When in doubt, shoot. If you shoot, make sure you kill.'"

Sheb asked, "What was that phone call about?"

"Command was pissed off that we didn't tell them what was going on, but that's for me and the captain to worry about, not you guys."

"How in the hell did they find out?"

"Someone on the team told them while we were conducting the ambush. Since it was nobody that was on the target, it had to be someone that stayed here at the team house. I'm sure if one thinks about it, I'm sure they can figure out for themselves who the snitch was." John stared at Jeff.

The room was silent; it was no big secret to anyone who had opened their mouth.

John continued. "Anyways, that's past and it's time to move on. Everyone is doing a fantastic job, and the stress meter seems a little high right now. So, I thought we might have a party! Tonight some girls are being brought in, and we are going to break open the beer and whiskey and blow off some steam with a party in the pool house."

John waited for a few minutes so he could watch everyone's expressions before he continued. "There are only two people on this team who are single, Eddie and myself. With that being said, you all know my policy. I don't care what you do as long as it doesn't affect the team's mission. So who wants to take part?" John asked.

Only four individuals said they wanted to take part: Eddie, Wally, Miguel, and John.

"Now, since that is settled, let's have the grill set up and some steaks cooked by 1900. The girls will be arriving at 2100. And one more thing—before you go to bed after the party tonight, make sure the place is cleaned up. The last thing we need is for the sergeant major to come by early in the morning and see this place covered with empty beer cans and whiskey bottles." John stood up, signaling the end of the meeting.

The rest of the day was uneventful; John spent it by going for a jog inside of the compound wall. The small track was only an eighth of a mile, but it was always easy for John to get lost in his own thoughts while running, and he usually ran for time, not distance. He could do the same thing on a treadmill; running for an hour was always an easy thing for him no matter what the course was. Many people had a hard time running on a track or a treadmill, and over the years John had gotten tired of listening to their excuses and complaints:

"I can't stand running on a treadmill."

"I can't run laps, going around and around."

"I'd rather lift weights."

"I don't think running is all that important."

"I like to run where the scenery changes."

And John's favorite, "We put to much emphasis on running."

He had laughed when he had heard that one. After someone said that John would pull out the last Army Physical Fitness Test, the team did and point out that only two people on the team scored a 300 on the last test: Eddie and himself. It wasn't the pushups or sit-ups that were the problem, but the run.

"According to the last results of the APFT, only two people got the maximum score on their tests. Only two people got a 100 on their run. So, that tells me we need to work on more running," John would announce. This statement usually shut everyone's mouth for a while, but every now and then someone would come back with a statement like, "I'm more into weight lifting, and I can bench press more weight than you."

John would laugh at this and comment, "Too bad the army doesn't require you to lift weights. Then maybe you could have some bragging rights. Until you get a perfect score on your APFT, you get no say in the team physical training program."

Blah, blah, blah. He would take all these excuses, comments, and complaints in stride because that's what they were—excuses. He also knew from experience that most people who complained about running weren't very good runners.

He was thirty minutes into his run when Sheb and Eddie joined him.

All three were quiet for five minutes before Sheb finally said, "Boss, are you sure this party is a good idea?"

"No, I'm not, but everyone deserves a break. What do you think Eddie?"

"I think it's a great idea. I told you out in Fallujah that I wanted some pussy," Eddie said as he pulled slightly ahead of the other two.

"Sheb, you're not going to give me a hard time during this whole run, are you?" John asked.

"Nah, Eddie and I just thought you were looking a little peaked out here. You're the oldest guy on the team, and we just wanted to be near in case you had a heart attack."

"Fuck you," John said, but he couldn't help but laugh.

At four in the afternoon John noticed several guys with beers in their hand already; starting a little early, he thought, but what the hell. He cracked a beer himself and took a long swig. Eddie approached him and asked, "Can I get one of those Viagra from you?"

John started laughing. "Having a little problem down there?"

"No, I just want to get my money's worth tonight," Eddie said, grinning.

John handed Eddie a Viagra and shook his head. It was going to be a wild night!

6

The team sat around the fire pit drinking beer. Eddie was taking a lot of ribbing from everyone else because he had already taken a Viagra pill.

Miguel said, "What if the girls don't show up? You're going to walk around all night with a hard-on."

"How do you know?" Eddie replied.

"It's Viagra. I heard it makes your dick hard for days."

Eddie was getting tired of people who talked about something like they were the experts, especially when they were basing their entire argument on hearsay. He stood up. "Has anyone here ever tried it?"

Nobody replied, so Eddie continued, "Since nobody here has tried it, you all need to shut the fuck up!"

Again there was silence.

John was smiling. Eddie's going to make a great team sergeant one of these days, he thought to himself.

The girls arrived promptly at 2100 hours. John was the first one out of his seat to greet them when they stepped out of the van, because he knew that a beast from hell could step out, and he didn't want to be the one stuck with her. As the girls filed out of the van, John spotted a young, beautiful woman and immediately held out his arm for her to take.

Seeing this, Eddie followed suit, grabbing the first thing that looked decent. He was glad he did this, because the next two out of the van—although not ugly, per se—were fat. One was not terribly obese, but the other was enormous.

The whole group moved to the pool house and the party was off and running. Over the next couple of hours, the team drank cases and cases of beer, and every once in a while someone would slip out with one of the girls, only to return an hour later for yet more beer.

John had had his fun with the young Iraqi girl and was now watching everyone have a good time. He noticed that nobody was messing with the fat one. He figured, what the hell, I'll take one for the team.

John noticed something else. Some of the guys who had said they weren't going to take part seemed to be getting awfully cozy with some of the girls. Fruit loops! His plan was working.

As the night wore on, John just sat in a dark corner of the pool house, leaning against the wall, sipping on a beer, and watching. He finally saw the opportunity he had been waiting for, and the number one reason for throwing this party.

Jeff, who had a nice, beautiful wife at home, was now floating around the pool with the youngest Iraqi girl, and both of them were naked. Jeff was so engrossed with the young lady that he didn't notice anything else around him, least of all John.

John watched for several minutes. When he was satisfied that he had what he needed, he decided to take the fat girl and make her earn her pay. As John was fucking the fat girl his only thought was, "Whoever invented Viagra should get the Nobel Peace Prize."

The girls left at 0400. As John was watching them leave, Eddie staggered up beside him and handed him a beer. "Boss, I want to be the first to thank you for the party, and to say you are the man for fucking that big fat chick."

"She wasn't that bad," John replied.

They both looked at each other and broke into drunken laughter. They sat down outside the pool house and watched the Tigris River flow slowly by. The moon was up, and it sparkled lightly off the surface of the water.

Eddie glanced at his watch and then the sky. "It's almost daylight."

John looked up and replied, "Yes it is. Is everyone else in bed?"

"Just you and me left, boss."

"Why don't you go to bed, and I'll clean this mess up," John said, looking at all the empty beer cans scattered everywhere.

"I thought you said you wanted everyone to clean up before they went to bed."

"I did, but you see how that turned out."

"I'll help you out, boss," Eddie said, grabbing a garbage bag.

The captain walked out onto the porch at 0500. He knew the party had lasted most of the night and didn't expect to see anyone moving, but there was John having a cup of coffee.

"Good morning, sir."

"Good morning, John. Well, how did the party go last night?"

"No problems, sir."

"What's the plan for today?"

"Today is maintenance day. We'll get all the inventories done, and then this afternoon we'll take Jeff to the B-team, Special Forces Company Headquarters," John said.

The captain leaned over. "How are you going to handle that?"

John handed the captain his digital camera. "Take a look at picture number three."

The captain looked at the picture and shook his head. "Too bad it had to come to this."

"Well sir, he brought it on himself. It's just insurance. If Jeff is any kind of a man, I won't have to use it," John said.

7

John confronted Jeff later that morning, "Sit down Jeff."

"You going to counsel me again?" Jeff asked in his well-known smart-ass tone.

"No, I'm going to fire you! After we're done here, you will go pack your gear and then we'll take you to the B-team, where the company sergeant major can decide what to do with you. But you will not spend another day on this team," John said.

"You can't fire me! I'm the best soldier on this team! Plus, I know so much about what this team has done. I would feel obligated to tell someone, especially about the party last night."

John hung his head and let out a breath of disgust. "You know, you really are a piece of shit! I thought you would say something like that. So let's talk about the party last night. You said that you were not going to take part, but you did. Am I right?"

"No, you're wrong! I didn't do anything last night," Jeff said, defensively.

John had had enough; only two members of the team had done absolutely nothing last night: Sheb and the captain. John didn't want to waste any more time, so he tossed out an eight by ten picture of Jeff with the Iraqi girl, both naked, in each other's arms, in the pool. He said, "I'm no genius, but that looks like you're doing something."

He didn't wait for a reply, but hammered his point home as Jeff stared at the picture. "You say you did nothing, so what you're doing in the pool with that young Iraqi girl is nothing? I wonder if you would do the same thing with a man, perhaps?"

"What are talking about?" Jeff said, deflated.

"If it really was nothing, as you claim, you would do the same thing with a man, right? You don't need to answer that. Let me put it this way. If your wife walked into the pool house at the same time I took this photo, do you think she would be mad? I mean, after all, you are doing nothing."

Jeff looked like he'd been punched in the gut. "I can't believe you're doing this."

"What the hell did you expect? You've been badmouthing people on this team for months and have caused nothing but problems. You get a pleasure out of stabbing people in the back. Hell, you just threatened me by saying you were going to blab about the party." John continued to let him have it. "Now let me tell you something. You will go work on the B-team and you will keep your mouth shut. I suggest you forget everything that ever happened on this team because I will show this picture to your wife, and you can explain to her that you were doing nothing."

"Are you threatening me, Sergeant?" Jeff said in a whisper.

"No, I'm promising you!" John said, and then added, "I suggest you take a long look in the mirror. You may be surprised at what you see, and hopefully you'll come to the conclusion that the root of all your problems is staring right back at you."

For once Jeff was at a loss for words, but finally he said, "Are we done?"

John replied, "No, we're not done. Before we take you to the B-team, you need to give Eddie fifty dollars for last night. You did take part, and you will pay like everyone else. And lastly, sit down with Sheb and sign the operations fund over to him. I want all your ties with this team severed. Now, go pack your gear. We leave for the Green Zone in two hours."

Part III
No Matter What the Cost

God gave men the urge and women the answer!

—*Al Bundy*

1

John met with the captain shortly after his talk with Jeff. "Well sir, we're down to nine guys now. Correction, eight, since Larry is too much of a coward to leave the team house and has proved that he is completely unreliable on the street."

They talked for several minutes about the way John had been forced to handle the situation with Jeff. They tried to brainstorm other ways in which they could have possibly handled it, but neither John nor the captain could come up with anything.

Blackmail your own teammate! It was a tough call, but they both agreed that they must stay focused on the most important things: the team and its mission. John swore he would do whatever it took to protect that.

The captain took a few minutes before replying, having just witnessed John Smith crush someone's confidence, destroy their self-esteem and send him whimpering away with his tail tucked between his legs. He wanted to pick his words carefully because there was no way in hell he wanted John Smith as an enemy.

"Don't you think you're being a little hard on Larry? Coward is kind of a callous word."

"No, sir, I don't. There are only two kinds of people when it comes to stress, those who focus, and those who fold. I think Al Pacino said that in the movie *The Devil's Advocate*, and I can't agree with him more. No truer words were ever spoken." John paused because the captain had leaned forward, clearly unconvinced by John's analogy.

"I don't think we can use a quote from an Al Pacino movie to explain the situation were in, even though I'm a big fan of his. Stress is one thing, but combat is completely different."

"I disagree, sir. Stress is stress, whether you're trying to meet a deadline by stocking shelves in a hometown grocery store or you find yourself moving through a narrow backstreet alley in a firefight," John stated.

The captain leaned back in his chair and chuckled. "That's not a very realistic comparison, and there's a big dissimilarity that you're overlooking."

"What's that, sir?"

"That stock boy in a grocery store is not going to turn a corner one day and walk into a hail of gunfire, or he won't be walking casually down the cereal aisle and suddenly lose his leg because he just stepped on a landmine. The soldier knows he could die at any minute on any given day, so I think your comparison is out of perspective."

"Sir, that's a great point, but what I'm saying is that stress is relative to whatever your job is. We're soldiers! We're at war! Death could come at anytime, and if a soldier can't handle that, he needs to get the hell out of the military and get a job as a stock boy."

"Okay," The captain said, "I understand somewhat, but calling him a coward is still a little rough."

"Well, sir, the next time we do an operation, you can be partnered with Larry. As long as you understand that if we get into another firefight and you and Larry have to maneuver down the street, you will find yourself all alone!"

"All right already, I get your point! So, what do you think? Do we need to fire Larry, too?" The captain asked.

"I think we can wait until we get back to the States. Larry may not be worth a fuck in a fight, but he can watch the radios and the team house while we're out and about. We can plan every mission from this time on with Larry staying here. What do you think, sir?"

"Sounds like a good plan, and I think we'll be able to operate just fine with only nine guys. For now we need to refocus our efforts and start concentrating on developing some of our sources into actionable intelligence."

The captain explained to John that they had to be more active in expanding their list of Iraqi sources that were willing to give up good information and get rid of those that have produced nothing of value. As it stood, the captain said, the team had only three sources that had ever given reliable information.

"I'd say we have four," John said.

The captain raised his eyebrows. "Who else is there?"

John explained. "Omar and his cousin. They came through for us on the enemy mortar crew. Let me try and work the situation and see if they can produce anything else for us. Omar's cousin has to have more knowledge about the insurgency. He was on the inside."

"Okay, that sounds good. Let's set a goal. Our goal is that in one month's time everyone on the team has found at least one source that is giving him actionable intelligence."

John thought for a minute, then concluded that this was a realistic goal. Some members of the team hadn't been to any school for this type of mission specifically, but they had had some training in the field of intelligence collection.

John wasn't worried about it; they were all smart enough to learn more on the job. Plus, if you broke down the whole spectrum of human intelligence collection, it was really all as simple as interviewing someone.

The whole collection process had many features. First you had to vet your source, to try to find out if you could trust them. But that part of the collection process had to be skipped in some cases because John's unit was only deployed for six months at a time. Real collection and development of a network of sources took years.

In John's experience, any source worth a shit would tell you right up front whether or not he had any good information, without any games. That's the type of informant they wanted, someone who was willing to stick his own neck out. People like Omar and his cousin.

The only hard part of the whole collection process was doing all the damn paperwork! The relationship between how much time a guy spent interviewing someone as opposed to how much time he spent filling out the paperwork as the result of that interview was staggering.

John despised paperwork, and also hated sitting behind a computer. Computers accomplished nothing but making paperwork pretty. In his opinion, there were only three quantifiable results when you fight the terrorists—only three questions someone should ask you when you finish your deployment:

One: How many guys did you kill?

Two: How many weapons did you confiscate?

Three: How many Iraqi soldiers did you train to the point where they can operate independently?

If you could answer these three questions with high numbers, then you knew you have made a significant impact on the terrorist organization and had taken the first step to winning.

As for the paperwork, John had figured it out one time. To conduct a simple one-hour operation, the team would have to spend a total of three hours doing paperwork. So if the team had followed the guidelines and done all the paperwork required for the simple ambush they conducted on the enemy mortar crew, it would have taken three hours of paperwork. And that's only if the mission got approved!

The captain interrupted John's daydream. "I say for the next few days we hang out at the FOB Falcon army base in the south of this city. There are always Iraqis coming in there with information. The army team that handles all of the 'walk-ins' is usually overworked, so maybe we can help out by taking some of the workload. Who knows, we may even find a couple of guys that can give us some decent intelligence."

John replied, "Damn good idea, sir. I hope they still have that smoothie shop on Falcon."

2

Eddie walked into the smoothie bar searching for John and immediately spotted him sitting at a corner table sipping on a strawberry smoothie and talking to a female soldier who couldn't have been over twenty years old.

He sat down and glanced at John, but quickly switched his attention to the young girl, taking a long, hard look at her. She had dishwater blonde hair and bright blue eyes, and even though she was wearing an army uniform, Eddie could tell she had a very good body hiding in there somewhere. He shook his head to knock himself out of the daze and said to John, "I think I found someone that will be perfect. I'll meet with him again in the morning."

John nodded, but didn't say anything in response to Eddie's comment. He knew Eddie had found an Iraqi man that looked to be a good source of information. Instead he introduced his companion.

"Eddie, this is Tanya. Tanya is a generator mechanic, and she just turned nineteen yesterday," John said proudly.

"Happy birthday, Tanya," Eddie said, raising his eyebrows at John.

"By the way Eddie, the base sergeant major was kind enough to lend us the use of a small building on the south side of the compound. You know, just in case we're down here late at night or we have an early morning meeting scheduled, we can just spend the night in the building. I've already swept the main crud out, but tomorrow when we come down for your meeting, we can bring some good cleaning supplies and do a better job sprucing it up."

Eddie was surprised. "Damn! How big is the building?" he asked.

"It's not that big. There are three rooms in the building. In two of the rooms we'll install a couple of beds for sleeping quarters, and the third we'll set up as an operations room. I was also lucky enough to procure a table and six chairs."

"Procure, huh?" Eddie smiled.

"I know we have an old TV and refrigerator at the team house that nobody uses, too. We can bring those along tomorrow, and we should be set up!"

Eddie looked at John, stunned. "I guess you've been busy all afternoon while I was in my meeting." He looked at Tanya, then back to John, and added, "Real busy!"

John just smiled. "Get yourself a smoothie for the road and we'll head back to the team house to get organized for tomorrow." He turned and looked at Tanya. "Tanya, it was a pleasure to meet you, and like I said before, if you're ready for your greatest adventure, I will see you tomorrow."

"Oh, you will definitely see me tomorrow," Tanya said as she got up to leave.

Eddie was just getting his smoothie when John walked up beside him at the counter. Eddie said, "You're amazing! You're old enough to be that girl's father! You cradle robber!"

"Number one, she is over eighteen, which is legal in any country. And two, she is only half my age, which is perfect. I was thinking she actually might be a little old for me, but I guess I can't be picky since we're in Iraq. She'll have to do!" John winked as he looked at Eddie.

They were still laughing as they headed out the door. The Iraqi that had served them the smoothies just shook his head and said, "*Amreeky magnooneen.*" Crazy Americans, indeed.

3

As Bruce was hooking up the TV, he was thankful the outlets in the building hadn't been ripped out, and that all the power for the building was hooked up to the base generators. This made it relatively easy to set up a suitable operations area. Even though this was his first deployment and he hadn't experienced worse firsthand, Sheb had told him horror stories about places that had no electricity. Sheb told him, for instance, about a time in Afghanistan, when the building they had occupied had been completely stripped of everything electrical, and he had had to start from scratch.

Having proper electricity always seemed to become the responsibility of the commo guy. For some reason everyone assumed that because the commo guy was trained in communications, that he also must be an electrician. Being the junior communications sergeant on the team, Bruce had prepared himself for this extra task with the guidance of Sheb, but still he was glad he didn't have to wire or rewire the little building.

Wally finished the last of the cleaning. He had cleaned both of the bedrooms from top to bottom with bleach water and ammonia. This left a strong smell, but at least the rooms were clean. Four beds that the team had purchased from an Iraqi local were already installed.

The rooms themselves were all the same size, about eight feet wide and twelve feet deep. They were not connected by any interior doors, but instead had separate entrances from the outside. As small as the building was, the team was grateful to have an extra place to hang out. With the few amenities they had added and everything cleaned up, it had become quite comfortable. Bruce even said, "We could just stay down here and conduct operations, make things a lot more convenient."

John and Sheb sat outside talking about the aftereffects the team was going through resulting from Jeff's firing. John told Sheb about the photograph he had used to blackmail Jeff into keeping his mouth shut, and Sheb told John about how Wally and Bruce had looked up to Jeff, and were shocked and somewhat pissed off at his firing.

"They will get over it, but that also proves another point and makes me believe I did the right thing," John said. He then asked Sheb, "Do you think Jeff was a good role model for these young guys?"

"Absolutely not. Personally, I hated that asshole, and I think you should have fired him a long time ago. I just wanted you to know what the feeling is on the team at large," Sheb said.

"Thanks, but these guys are young. Like I said, they'll get past it." John pointed down the street. "Here comes Eddie, and judging by how fast he's walking, he must have gotten some good information from his source."

Eddie approached, looking excited. "Boss, we need to act fast. My source says he knows where there are two hostages being held."

The three went inside to hear Eddie tell his story. Eddie's source had explained that an Indian truck driver and an Egyptian truck driver were being held hostage in his neighborhood. The source had seen both the hostages from the window of his house. He knew who they were from a news report that he had heard. Both hostages were bound with their hands behind their back. Neither hostage had a hood on, but both were blindfolded. They had been brought there last night and were being held by four people. All four of the kidnappers had been carrying AK-47s.

Eddie had showed his source a map of the city, and the man indicated where his house was located and the building where the hostages were being held. They were right beside one another. Realizing the buildings were only two miles from FOB Falcon, Eddie thought that if they acted quickly they could get out there within the hour.

John agreed.

Eddie went on to explain that he had sent his source home with a cell phone. The source had said he could see the entire building where the hostages were being held, including the front and rear exits. Eddie had given him instructions to call every fifteen minutes with updates, or to call sooner if anything significant happened.

When Eddie had finished his narrative, John leaned back in his chair, lost in thought. Sheb was concerned—John never had to think these things through. It was obvious to everyone what the course of action should be. They had to go get them. On the other hand, Sheb knew John well enough to realize that maybe something else was at play here.

John tipped his chair forward. "Eddie, you call the captain. Give him a summary of what's going on. Tell him to bring Miguel and get down here. It should only take them about a half hour, so if your source does what he's supposed to do, we should have two updates on the hostages by the time Miguel and the captain get down here."

As Eddie moved to call the captain, John added, "Also, tell them to bring the M79 grenade launcher."

John continued, to Sheb, "While Eddie is talking to the captain, I need everyone else to double check their gear. Don't let anyone get too relaxed, because we may leave at any time. You should be ready within one minute to roll out the gate."

John turned his attention back to the map, spreading it out for all to see, and they began to plan their route. John allowed Wally and Bruce to get involved in the planning process; he let them pick the primary and alternate routes to the target. He sat back and observed as they did this. He hoped that by getting them more involved in the planning process, they would feel like a bigger part of the team, and maybe they'd start to forget about Jeff, or see how fucked up he really was.

Wally suddenly looked up. "We have the route."

John listened carefully as they explained the routes to the target that they had come up with. When they finished, John said, "That's a good job, but what about the return route?"

Wally and Bruce looked at each other, and this time it was Bruce who spoke. "If we take the primary route to the target, we can use the alternate route when we return, or vice-versa."

John said, "That sounds real good, an excellent job. Let me add something you may want to consider. Suppose—just suppose—there are some bad guys sitting right outside the walls of this compound, and their only job is to watch the gates, observing who comes and goes. Recording the departure and arrival times of military and civilian vehicles, how many vehicles, what types of vehicles, what type of armament on each vehicle, and which direction they go. Their only job is to try and establish movement patterns. We all know that nobody has more fixed patterns than Americans. These bad guys see us leave this army base in our civilian vehicle, then we rescue the hostages and return here."

John paused. He could tell by Wally's expression that he understood. Wally said, "If we rescue the hostages, we need to go the opposite direction. Maybe take them to the Green Zone or even to the team house. If we return here and we are spotted, our vehicle will be compromised, and we might as well have done the operation with a Hummer."

John smiled. "That's it! Why don't you plan a route to the Green Zone and another one to the team house, and we can decide which route to take if we rescue the hostages."

John let Wally and Bruce go back to the planning because Eddie had just got off the phone with the captain.

"Captain Rinehart said he would call back before they leave," Eddie hardly had a chance to say before his cell phone started ringing.

Everyone immediately looked up because they knew that this was Eddie's source with the first update. Even Sheb, who was half asleep in his chair, sat up straight with anticipation.

All eyes were on Eddie as he talked with his source. John was thankful that the source could speak decent English. When an interpreter was used, so many details were lost in the translation, not to mention the amount of time wasted in repeating the same thing over several times. But the biggest problem with interpreters, in John's opinion, was, were they really saying what you told them to say? Unless you had a good grasp of the language yourself, there was no way to tell.

Eddie hung up the phone and gave a quick update on the situation. His source had arrived at home and now was casually observing the house where the hostages were being held. He said that there were currently only three guys guarding the hostages, and he had no idea where the fourth guy was. Eddie's source had also described the target house as being a one-story building with no wall surrounding it. The house was ten meters by ten meters, basic rectangle shape, and had two doors. The front door faced the main street, and the other door was on the back right corner of the building and opened into a small alley which was only accessible by foot traffic.

"No more than six rooms in the house," Eddie said. Before he could continue, Bruce spoke up, "How do you know it is six rooms or less?"

"Because of the size of the building, ten meters by ten meters, or thirty by thirty feet, one story. Basic Iraqi construction, definitely no more than six rooms, but more than likely only five."

Even John was impressed by this calculation; Eddie had an eye for dimensions. John could punch himself for being so stupid; he had been in enough homes in Iraq to be an expert on their construction, but the thought of memorizing the basic layouts and sizes had never occurred to him. Eddie was the man!

Now the team knew what the house looked like, where it was located, and what the opposition consisted of. The only thing remaining was to wait for the captain and Miguel to arrive.

John tried to think of anything else they could do while they waited. His cell phone, which was normally off, began to buzz. He thought that if he left his cell phone on all the time, people call him all the time, but in his mind the phone was for just in case *he* needed something.

"Hello," John said.

"This is the captain."

"Are you on your way sir?"

"Not yet, I'm still waiting on clearance from the B-team."

John stood up suddenly and walked outside to talk with the captain privately.

"Sir, are you telling me that you briefed Command on the hostage situation?" John asked.

"Since we just got our asses chewed the other night for not keeping them informed, I figured this time we had better tell them what's going on, so I sent them a Con-op briefing."

John felt like crying because he knew he had screwed up, but only said, "Okay sir, I understand. I'll talk to you later."

Sheb could tell something was wrong from the expression on John's face as he walked back into the room. He asked, "What's going on?"

"Captain sent a Con-op to the B-team."

Sheb and Eddie looked at each other and dropped their heads with looks of defeat.

Bruce and Wally were in the dark. Bruce asked, "What are we missing?"

Sheb answered because he knew John was too mad to talk about it. "It means we're not going after the hostages, that's what it means!"

Bruce and Wally looked at each other, still confused, and Eddie added, "They will never approve us to go after the hostages."

Wally said, "I'm sure they'll approve this. We are so close to the target location, and there are only three bad guys guarding them."

Eddie laughed. "That's your way of thinking because you're down here on the ground. Unfortunately, the decision will be made by someone who has no idea what's going on in the street."

John finally spoke, "I want to apologize to everyone; this is all my fault." He looked over at Wally and Bruce and continued, "I can tell you exactly what's going to happen. The captain informed the B-team what's going on because he wanted to do the right thing. The B-team will also want to do the right thing, so they will pass the information to a higher Command. The information will continue going up the chain until it finally gets to the approving authority, and like Eddie said, that person doesn't have a clue on what's happening out here. They, in turn, will disapprove of us going after the hostages. Somewhere in the upper levels of Command a decision will finally be made to pass this to another unit, probably Delta Force—but the unit is irrelevant. Whatever unit gets the mission will ask us for all the intelligence that Eddie has accumulated, and they will do the hit."

John stopped talking, and Bruce spoke up, "That doesn't sound so bad, as long as someone does the hit."

"That is true," John continued, "Unfortunately, whoever does make the decision doesn't realize that time is the biggest issue on the street. The unit that does get the mission will take some time getting organized, and then they will have to travel down here. It could be as late as tomorrow, and by then the hostages may or may not be there, or they could be dead. I feel the hostages will be the ones to suffer."

Bruce asked, "If the decision-making process is too slow, why doesn't someone tell the higher levels of Command?"

Eddie broke in. "I'll tell you why! The only people with the balls to say something are the guys on the team, and our opinions never get past the Company level."

"I still don't understand. If something is broke, why won't they fix it?"

"Because, Bruce," John said calmly, "People are scared of losing their jobs."

John got up and stretched. "Now, I'm going in the next room to take a nap. Wake me up at 1200 hours, or if by some miracle they approve the mission."

Eddie said, "I'll stay in contact with my source, continue to get updates. I'll wake you if something comes up."

John nodded as he left the room. He felt the deflation of adrenalin and knew everyone else felt it, too.

4

"John, wake up!" Eddie said as he pounded on the door.

John rolled over and looked at his watch, 1100 hours. He had been sleeping for only an hour, and even though he felt completely refreshed, he longed for that second hour.

Then he realized something must have happened; Eddie wouldn't have woken him early without good reason.

John walked into the operations room and quickly noticed that Sheb and Wally were gone. Bruce was studying the map, and Eddie was on the phone. John sat down and yawned, waiting patiently for Eddie to finish his phone call. By the contents of the conversation, John could tell he was talking to his source.

When Eddie got off the phone, he brought John up to speed on the last hour's activities. Sheb and Wally had gotten bored with sitting around, so they went to the smoothie bar. The captain had called and given them the word; they were right about what was going to happen. Command had disapproved their Con-op. The mission was given to another unit, but they wouldn't be down there for another four hours.

This gave John a glimmer of hope; maybe they would get here in time—this time. But his excitement was quickly shot down when Eddie said, "I just got done talking with my source. The fourth guy has returned to the house where the hostages are being held, and it looks like they are getting ready to pack up and relocate."

They had to act quickly. Terrorists loved to move their hostages around frequently, which kept the Americans from homing in on their location. Every terrorist was worried that if they stayed in the same place long enough, the Americans would eventually find them.

John called the captain and said, "Sir, if we don't go now, I'm afraid the hostages will be moved and we'll miss our chance!"

"We can't, damn it! I have orders to stand down. Pass all the information you got to whatever unit shows up at your location this afternoon." John could tell by the captain's tone that he was just as frustrated.

Eddie looked over at John with questioning eyes, and when John just shook his head, Eddie knew they were fucked. Actually, it was the hostages who were fucked!

But John didn't want to give up, so he called directly to the B-team to plead the case. He emphasized how time was the most critical part of this mission, not who conducted it or who got credit for it.

Again Eddie could tell by his expression that John was being told to stand down. Sheb and Wally had returned from the smoothie bar just in time to hear the contents of John's conversation with the B-team. John folded up his cell phone and stuck it in his pocket. He sat still, a defeated look on his face.

Sheb said, "Now what?"

"Now, Eddie continues to talk with his source and receive updates. The rest of us sit on our asses and wait for the unit that's supposed to be here this afternoon," John said, in almost a whisper.

Bruce pulled a movie out of his pack and slipped into the computer, saying, "Might as well watch a movie while we wait."

Sheb said, "Good idea. What is it?"

"*The Mountain Men*. Charlton Heston and Brian Keith."

John leaned back to watch the movie, one of his favorites. But when the movie started, he had trouble staying focused on it. This whole hostage business was eating away at him.

Bottom line in his mind: he had screwed up! The minute they had found out about the hostages, he should have taken the four guys that were with him and gone after them, not gotten on the phone and called someone.

He always thought that was the biggest problem in his unit. The first thing that occurred to most people when there was a problem was to call someone else and let them deal with it. It was funny; this was one of the rules John lived by.

Years earlier, he had started to notice a subtle difference between the soldiers of his unit. It was about being tough! Not strong, not fast; you could be the epitome of physical perfection, but were you tough?

John's buddy, Ray, was a perfect example of toughness.

Ray was working on the roof of his house one day, replacing the shingles with lifetime-warranty, green-colored tin. The sheets of tin were three feet wide and over ten feet in length, so handling them would be a tough task for two men, let alone one.

While muscling one sheet of metal over the crown of the roof, a gust of wind suddenly came up and twisted the sheet from Ray's grasp. In doing so it knocked him off balance, and he slid down the roof, falling to the concrete driveway below.

The distance was no more than ten feet, but Ray stuck out his arm instinctively to break his fall. The impact was too much, and his arm snapped like a twig. Although the break was bad, it didn't tear open the skin; a three-inch bump was immediately evident between his wrist and his elbow.

Ray took a second to catch his breath, then struggled to his feet and went searching for his wife to take him to the hospital. They owned a horse ranch covering a hundred acres, so it took Ray a half hour to locate his wife. She was in the process of exercising a horse when Ray approached her with his broken arm. She was justifiably horrified on seeing his arm, which was now starting to turn black from the trauma.

Did she drop what she was doing and rush him to the hospital? No!

Ray told her to put the horse up in a stall, first. The horse had cost thirty thousand dollars, and in Ray's mind it had priority over his shattered arm. It was forty-five minutes before Ray's wife was ready to take him to the hospital. Ray was now sweating from the pain, but still remained stoic.

The closest hospital was in Clarksville, Tennessee; normally an hour drive from their ranch, but his wife did it in thirty-five minutes. After x-rays, twisting, tweaking, and some good drugs, Ray's arm was set and a cast was put on.

That evening Ray had called John and told him the story. John thought it was funny, and now that the pain had subsided so did Ray, and they laughed together. Ray asked John if he could come help hang drywall in the morning. Of course, John said he would.

John arrived at Ray's house at nine in the morning, and to his surprise, Ray had already hung eight sheets of drywall with his broken arm. John shook his head and said, "You know that you are insane, right?"

Ray's reply was simple. "It's just a broken arm. That's why I got two!"

John loved telling that story, especially to men who whined about the littlest of things. But on hearing the story most people would say, "That sounds stupid!"

Everyone knows there is an ultra-thin line between stupidity and toughness. John has always said that Ray was the toughest SOB he had ever known, as did a few other people. Those who said it sounded "stupid" were the same ones who whined about something as small as a blister on their foot—or no air conditioning.

These were the differences John had started to see as the years passed. As he saw more, he made a list of them and adopted them as rules to live by. He called his list 'The difference between a Green Beret and a Special Forces soldier."

To his memory, John had just broken one of those rules:

Special Forces—When something is broken his first thought is, "Who can I call to get this fixed?"
Green Beret—When something is broken his first thought is, "How can I fix this?"

Upon further reflection, John realized he had actually broken two of his rules. The other one was:

Special Forces—Tries to do the right thing.
Green Beret—Does whatever it takes to get the job done.

John's list of rules to live by had grown to include twenty items over the years. He told himself that he would have to sit down one of these days and review the list again to make sure he was on the right track. He had already screwed up and broken two; how many more might he have broken?

John also realized that he probably needed to share this list with the guys on his team, since a few of them had already broken one of the rules:

Special Forces—Cheats on his wife while on deployment.
Green Beret—Doesn't cheat on his wife, ever.

When John finally shifted his attention back to the movie, it had been playing for an hour. John watched Charlton Heston being chased by a band of Blackfoot Indians. He had escaped initial capture by hiding inside a beaver dam. The Indians tried to search the beaver dam; they had even sent out one brave to inspect it, but Heston killed him with a spear that the Indians had been kind enough to give him before his death run. Now that's close-quarters combat!

John had always wondered what it would be like to have fought in those times. The guns were black powder, muzzle loaders, which meant you had better make damn sure of that first shot because more than likely, your enemy would be on you before you had time to reload. Then it was down to the knife, a very personal way of killing, and very satisfying. *The Mountain Man* men—now those were some tough men!

John noticed Eddie's absence. Eddie was outside, pacing back and forth while talking to his source again. When he walked back into the room, he told Bruce to pause the movie. Judging by Eddie's expression it was not good news.

"My source said the kidnappers just took off with the hostages."

John stood up scowling viciously, but didn't say anything. Sheb was somewhat scared at the look on John's face, but just as quickly John's face softened and he smiled. No point in being mad; he had done all the right things. But next time, he promised himself, he'd get the job done.

John started to walk out of the room. Sheb called after him, "Where the hell you going?"

He didn't even turn around to reply, "I'm going to see if I can find that nice, young girl I met yesterday."

Sheb watched John walk out into the street and head for the middle of the base. Behind him, Bruce said, "Now what?"

Eddie answered, "Now we call everyone and tell them the hostages have been moved and we have no idea where. The operation will be cancelled. I'll set up another meeting with my source for the morning, and we'll start over all over again."

Wally said, "This sucks!"

Bruce looked at Sheb and spoke. "Sheb, you have known John for a long time. Why did he say that this was his fault?"

Sheb replied, "John knew by telling the captain about the mission, the captain would then tell the B-team. Things would continue to go up the chain until finally it got high enough for someone to make a decision." He paused. "Remember the old saying, 'Keep it simple?' That saying applies to this situation, if you think about it. The more moving parts you have, the harder they are to keep in sync. Also, the more moving parts you have, the more likely something will break."

Sheb went on. "John knew this, and he also knew the simplest way to solve this hostage situation was for us five to drive out there, kill the bad guys, and rescue the hostages. It would have been that simple."

Wally then asked, "How did he know all this was going to happen?"

"Because it had happened before, one year ago this month. Back then John was on ODA 453." Sheb told them the story …

5

Nasiriyah, Iraq: 2003

John sat on the hood of the Hummer cleaning his M24 bolt-action sniper rifle, a daily routine he loved. No matter if he had fired it or not, he ran a clean patch through the barrel every day and wiped off the bolt.

This was the first time in his military career that he was able to work exclusively as a sniper, and it was all thanks to his understanding team sergeant.

When John had first come into the army he had set two simple goals for himself. One was to become a sergeant; the other was to be a sniper. Both of the goals had been relatively simple to achieve. He was now a sergeant first class, and he had killed many people using the sniper rifle.

He had been busy with his sniper rifle since infiltrating Iraq in the middle of the night on the 18th of March, 2003. In fact, the team had gotten into a big firefight the day the war actually started, just two days later.

On that day his skills as a sniper were put to the test. He had taken shots from distances of one hundred meters to one thousand meters. He knew he'd missed a couple of times and wasn't afraid to admit it, but he figured his bullet-to-kill ratio was about 80 percent. Statistics were never his strong point, though, so he didn't know if 80 percent was good or bad.

But one thing he did know was that he was having the time of his life, jumping from rooftop to rooftop and slipping unnoticed through the dark alleys of Nasiriyah. No helmet, no body armor, no bulky equipment—what a rush!

But now, after the weapon was cleaned to his satisfaction, John leaned back on the front window of the Hummer to watch the activities around him. The team had been staying in an old goat barn for the last week. The barn was owned by the local sheik, who had been hiding out in Jordan for the last ten years. They brought this sheik with them when they came into country, and now the sheik was back in business.

John estimated that fifty to seventy-five people came to see the sheik every day. They mostly came for favors; the sheik was the local Godfather. If you wanted anything done around the town of Nasiriyah, you came to the sheik.

An added bonus to all these people coming to visit the sheik was that many wanted to talk with the Americans. It was funny to John; it seemed every person had important information that would save the world. John would watch this with interest. Other members of the team were tasked with the collection of intelligence, not him, so he could sit back and relax until he was needed for an operation.

But things changed dramatically that day. As John was sitting on the hood half asleep, an Iraqi male approached him. Normally John wouldn't even bother talking with Iraqis who came up to him but would immediately point out one of the other members of the team and send the Iraqi in their direction.

Today he was bored, however, so he decided to hear what the Iraqi had to say. The man told John that there were Americans being held at the hospital in town. John asked him a few more questions, and it seemed like the guy knew what he was talking about. He even gave the name of a female John knew to be missing.

John knew this was important, so he quickly took the Iraqi and introduced him to another member of the team who was really good at getting detailed information from an Iraqi source. Within the hour it was clear to everyone that the team had, in fact, just found some Americans that had gone missing. The team sergeant informed Command, which was still back in Kuwait, and gave them all the details of the situation.

Meanwhile the team continued to collect more information, and by the second day John finally asked what the hell were they waiting for. He thought to himself, why aren't we going to rescue them?

They didn't go because the team had been told to stand down and continue to collect intelligence. John knew what was going on; he remembered a similar situation in Somalia.

After four days of sitting on their asses, an Iraqi came up to John and asked why they had not gone to the hospital to rescue the Americans. He said, "These are your own people, don't you care?"

John had no reply to this.

The Iraqi then told him that the only people left at the hospital were some staff members, because all the bad guys had disappeared into the general population. They had gotten scared because some helicopters had over flown the hospital.

John thought, why were helicopters flying over the hospital? Some commander trying to get a look at the objective?

There would be no reason for alerting the bad guys by flying helicopters over the objective, because the team had sent pictures back. The team had even put a hidden camera on the Iraqi source, who then went to the hospital and filmed the interior layout for them. All the intelligence was already collected; so why the helicopters?

The Iraqi even went on to tell John that some of the hospital staff had even tried to deliver the female hostage to the Americans, in an ambulance. On approaching a military checkpoint, the Americans had fired upon the ambulance and they had to return to the hospital.

A realization swept over John. "Wait a minute! I thought you said there were two Americans alive?"

"There were!" the Iraqi said.

That evening there was a televised rescue for the whole world to see.

A couple of things about this whole situation really pissed John off. One, there were two Special Forces teams within ten minutes of the hospital, yet they did nothing. According to the source, there had been two Americans alive at one point, but only one was rescued from the hospital.

It ate at John hard because he could only wonder, if they had gone the first day they received the information, could they have been able to save someone else? He had never been able to confirm this. He had only the source's word that there had been two hostages. John didn't doubt this source's information because all the information he had given them before had turned out to be true. There was no real reason to doubt the presence of two hostages, but he still was never able to fully confirm it.

The second thing that pissed John off was that all the bad guys had left the area by time the rescue was executed. This may have been a good thing for the American rescuers because there was no opposition left in the hospital. But the fact was that the bad guys were still out on the streets, and sooner or later someone would have to deal with them. They hadn't just gone back to their families and quit being terrorists. They would continue to go after and kill more Americans.

John went to the hospital the morning after the rescue. He was able to talk with some of the hospital staff, and after getting their side of the story John had a complete story of what had happened. The only portion he was missing was why two Special Forces A-teams had been told to stand down. He had a good guess, but that information would have to wait until they were pulled out of Iraq.

He sat on the hood of a Hummer watching the bustling of activity that now surrounded the hospital, wondering at the thought process that had led to this. To him, it was so simple:

When Americans are in danger, you go! You don't analyze, you don't think about it. You just go after them and kill all the bad guys! So why were the Special Forces teams told to stand down? Was it a lack of assets?

It turned out that the two Special Forces teams had at their disposal: four Hummer gun trucks, each with a crew-serve gun and thousands of rounds of ammunition for each gun. Twenty Special Forces soldiers who had all been extensively trained in close-quarter combat. A dedicated AC130 Spectra gun ship—a heavily armed aircraft capable of placing accurate fire in any weather from an elevation of eight thousand feet—to guide them in and out of town. Plus, an Iraqi source on the inside who had given them the complete layout of the hospital.

So why were they told to stand down?

The eighty-sixth hospital unit was set up at Taleel Air Base, which was a fifteen-minute drive from Nasiriyah. They could have easily driven the wounded there, where they would have received the best medical treatment available. Not to mention that there was a Marine Expeditionary Unit also set up on the outskirts of Nasiriyah, which could have easily secured the whole area around the hospital after the rescue.

So why stand down?

On returning to Kuwait after six months in Iraq, John decided to find the answer to that question. After talking with five high-ranking officers and three sergeant majors, John had received two answers.

Two of the sergeant majors had said, "I don't know."

The five officers and the third sergeant major gave the following answer: "The decision was made at a very high level, and the mission was given to a specific unit to justify the unit's existence and its inflated budget." That was the answer!

6

"So, John always vowed that he wouldn't let that happen again. In fact, he said he would risk his job, a court-martial, or even jail instead of sitting back and doing nothing," Sheb said, finishing the story.

Wally said, "But they had been told not to go in by Command."

Sheb responded, "John doesn't see it that way. He blames himself for not at least trying."

"But he was just following orders!"

"Yes, he was, but imagine if you were laid up wounded, being held by terrorists in a shit-hole hospital, and then finally someone came to rescue you. But afterwards, you found out there were two Special Forces A-teams that knew where you were, but they did nothing. How would that make you feel?"

"Like shit! I would definitely want to know why they did nothing."

Sheb nodded. "I will tell you this for nothing: if Eddie's source locates the truck drivers again, John will go after them—by himself if he has to."

Bruce chimed in. "Damn, that's one hell of a story. I had read the story about what had taken place in Nasiriyah, but I'd never heard what had happened behind the scenes."

Sheb stood up and said, "Nobody knows, and nobody wants to hear about it, either. Do you think that the young girl who was rescued knows that someone left her to rot in that hospital for days, and that her kidnappers are walking around free to this day?"

"Well, if she does know, it's got to make her feel like shit."

"Ask John about it sometime, he'll be more than happy to give you the details. He feels so responsible that he has always said that if he ever meets her, he would apologize for his inaction."

"That's a little extreme," Wally said. "I don't see how he can blame himself."

"Like I said, ask him about it. I do know that the only people who know exactly what happened are the people that were there. So, with that said, I'm going to go find John, and see if we're spending the night down here."

Eddie added, "My source wants to meet at 0600, so I think we'll be staying. I'll call the captain again and let him know we'll be spending the night here."

Then everyone's attention was diverted as a civilian truck pulled up and stopped in front of the building. Sheb walked out to see who it was.

John stepped out of the passenger side of the vehicle and motioned for Sheb to come help him. He dropped the tailgate and handed Sheb two cases of Corona beer. "Put these in the fridge, will ya?"

Sheb took the beer inside while John talked for a few minutes to the civilian that had given him a ride.

When he came inside, everyone was staring at him. Sheb asked the obvious: "Where in the hell did you get the beer?"

John replied, "One of the civilian contractors that works on this base as an electrician remembered me from when we met in Afghanistan. We got to talking, and I managed to weasel a couple cases of beer out of him." John looked at each of the guys. "So, I think we should relax all afternoon, watch a few movies, and have a couple of beers. Any objections?"

Of course, nobody objected.

"Man, I love this team," Wally said.

The guys sat back and watched several movies, sipped on a few beers, and generally wasted the whole afternoon away. During this hang-out session they discussed what had transpired, and generally bitched about having their hands tied. John just sat and listened, and finally Eddie said something that summed up the whole situation. "I would hate to be a hostage in this country!"

John looked at Eddie and said, "I think the hostages will be back at the same house in the morning."

Eddie raised his eyebrows in question.

John continued, "This is just a guess on my part, but if the hostages survive the night, I think the kidnappers will return to their house. It is my theory that they will try and ransom the hostages tonight, since these guys were just kidnapped a few days ago. I think the kidnappers are just proving they have the hostages, and tonight they will make their demands. They'll wait a few days, and if their demands are not met, the hostages will be killed."

Before anyone could speak John said, "I realize there are a lot of 'ifs' in this theory; that's why it's just a theory. The kidnappers could have another house where they could hold the hostages. Plus, they may kill them tonight, but I have a hunch that they will try and get money first. You guys know as well as I do that money trumps everything in life. These terrorists may claim they have a cause for Allah, but if you a throw a trunk full of money in front of them, they will gladly embrace every infidel in the world and convert to Christianity before the money is counted."

Eddie chimed in, "That is a fact. Everyone does have a touch of greed in them, but even if they don't return to the same house, I'm still hopeful that my source will find out something tomorrow that will help us."

"Let's keep our fingers crossed. As for tonight, I think some of us will be busy." John gave Eddie a wink as he settled in to watch another movie.

There was a knock on the door at 2000 hours. They could tell by the lightness of the tapping that it was a woman. Eddie looked over at John with a questioning look on his face. John just smiled and stood up to answer the door.

In walked Tanya and another girl, who was introduced as Shelly. Shelly was taller than Tanya and had jet-black hair which was pinned up because both women were in uniform, but they all could tell that when she let it down it would fall to the middle of her back. After the introductions were made, John sat down and Tanya settled in on his lap. Shelly walked over and sat beside Eddie. The two started up a conversation.

Wally and Bruce looked at each other and Wally whispered to Bruce, "John was gone for only three hours, and he comes back with a couple of cases of beer and two American women!"

The girls grabbed some beer and really settled in. The conversation was light-hearted and friendly. Eddie had immediately hit it off with Shelly, and they appeared to have a lot in common.

Or maybe Shelly was just horny!

Sheb seemed to ignore the girls; the only thing these girls did for him was make him miss his wife.

The girls had only been there for fifteen minutes when John stood up and said, "I'll see you guys in the morning." He took Tanya into one of the bedrooms.

Eddie spent the next thirty minutes talking with Shelly before she suddenly stood up, took Eddie's hand, and led him to the second bedroom.

Wally said, "This is great! Where the hell are we supposed to sleep?"

Bruce was also irritated. "This is fucked up!"

Yawning, Sheb said, "Grab a blanket. All three of us are sleeping on the floor in this room." Stretching out on the floor he added, "You two need to shut your mouths and quit acting so selfish."

"John and Eddie are the ones being selfish, by hogging both the bedrooms," Wally said.

"You know, Wally, sometimes you're an idiot! Let me ask both of you a question. Did either one of you thank John for that party at the team house the other night?"

The room was silent.

"I thought not. John risked his career to make sure you guys had a good time and you didn't even thank him. You probably didn't even help him clean up, did you?"

They remained silent.

"We married guys, we'll walk off the plane in a couple of months and into the arms of our waiting wives. Our kids will grab us around the legs and hang on with all the love a child can muster. When we go home we'll spend all day playing with the children, and be extremely grateful we survived a combat tour. That night our wives will make love to us like they did on the honeymoon."

Sheb yawned again before continuing, "John and Eddie will have no one to meet them, and they'll probably spend the first night back in the United States all by themselves. Neither one has any family. Think about that for a few minutes before you complain about sleeping on the floor. As married men, we have to make small allowances for the single guys because they make big allowances for us."

Wally stared at the ceiling. He had never thought of it like that. Now he remembered that when they had been prepping for deployment to Iraq, John had made sure that all the married men had plenty of time off to spend with their wives and children.

One day in particular, the team room was a mess; they had all their equipment laid out for inventory. So much gear was spread out on the floor that it left no room to walk. It was the late afternoon when John released them; he told everyone to go home. Everybody was glad to get off early and spend the extra time with his family. John and Eddie had remained, working halfway into the night. In the morning when everyone came back to work, they were shocked that the team room was spic-and-span, and all the equipment had been inventoried and packed neatly into their deployment boxes.

Wally did feel a little selfish. John and Eddie came to Iraq two weeks before anyone else on the team as the advance party. They had set everything up in preparation for the rest of the team. This had allowed the other guys two more weeks at home with their families. He also knew that John and Eddie would stay a couple of weeks after everyone else redeployed back to the States as the stay behind party, just to close everything out and make a smooth transition for their replacements.

7

Eddie was roused from sleep at 0530 by his cell phone's rings. As he reached for his phone, he looked beside him at the beautiful, naked woman, still sound asleep. He made a mental note to thank John for setting this up for him.

"Hello."

"Mr. Eddie, the hostages are back in the house."

"Call back in fifteen minutes and give me an update. *Maa salaamah.*" (Goodbye)

Eddie took a long look at the naked body beside him. She was absolutely stunning; she even looked better this morning than she had last night, if that was possible. He could sure use a quickie this morning, but business came first.

He nudged her on the shoulder. "Wake up, beautiful, it's time to go." Eddie stood up and quickly got dressed.

Shelly looked at Eddie with sleepy eyes. "Don't I get any coffee this morning?"

Eddie leaned over and kissed her. "I promise I'll make it up to you, but I got a feeling we'll be going out this morning to conduct an operation, so I owe you a rain check."

"Hmmm, you owe me a lot more than that," She said, stretching and grinning.

Eddie reluctantly left Shelly so she could dress while he went to wake up John. He noticed John squatting against the wall drinking coffee upon walking out of his room.

John raised his head. "Good morning, Eddie. Judging by your smile, I expect your night was good. I heard the phone ring; is it what I think it is?"

Eddie said, "Good morning, boss. Yep, they're back at the same house and my source has his eyes on it. He'll be calling back with an update in fifteen minutes."

John stood up and stretched. "Okay. Wake up the guys and get them ready. I'll get rid of Tanya."

Before John went back into the bedroom to wake Tanya, Eddie stopped him. "Boss, thanks for last night."

John answered haphazardly and waved Eddie off like it was no big deal. "You're welcome."

Sheb had heard the noise John and Eddie were making and walked outside to see what was going on. Eddie told him the situation.

"Are we supposed to call the captain or Command?" Sheb asked.

Shrugging his shoulders, Eddie said, "John didn't say anything, and after yesterday's fiasco I'm going to assume no."

Wally and Bruce were stirring and stretching, trying to get the kinks out of their bodies from having to sleep on the floor. "I hope I'm getting up this early for a reason," Wally said, stomping his foot to get the circulation back.

John made sure the girls got on their way. When he walked into the operations room everyone was wide awake and waiting in anticipation. "Eddie, how long before your source calls back?"

"About five minutes."

"John, how in the hell are you always right? You knew they would be back at the same house," Wally asked.

"You forget the first few weeks we were here. Remember how many hits we went on that turned out to be 'dry holes?' Quite a few! If you count up the times I've been right and compare it to the times I've been wrong, you'll see that I've been wrong more often. However, this time I was right. Sometimes you just get lucky!"

He smiled at Wally, but as quickly as the smile appeared it disappeared. John said with a serious look on his face, "If Eddie's source gives us the green light we are going to take the van and try a rescue. If we can get these guys, we'll take the hostages straight to the Green Zone. This is the important part; no matter what happens we all have to keep our mouths shut. If someone finds out about it, I will take full responsibility and accept the consequences. We all saw what happened yesterday, and I refuse to let that happen again. If you feel uncomfortable about this, you can stay here and there will be no hard feelings. Think about this before you make your decision—if it was you being held hostage, would you want someone like us to come rescue you?"

Wally and Bruce both answered together. "Let's go!"

Sheb said nothing; he just gave a thumbs-up.

John looked around the room and said, "Just to make sure, you guys are all absolutely certain about this? We could all get in serious trouble, and I can't guarantee my protection will mean anything to the Command."

Eddie put his hand on John's shoulder and said, "We're with you boss."

"Alright. I say we lock this building up and sit in the van waiting for the phone call from Eddie's source," John said proudly. He was happy that everyone was committed to getting the job done, and he couldn't be more proud of them for the risks they were willing to take with him.

Still, he was a little concerned. In the back of his mind he knew that there was no way in hell they could keep this operation a secret. Not with five guys. It was hard enough to keep a secret with just two people.

John didn't care. He could not stand by and do nothing—not this time.

Before everyone could get into the van, Eddie's phone rang. While he talked with the source he looked over at John and gave him nod of affirmation with his head. Game on!

Eddie gave them the details as the drove through the base gate. "All four kidnappers are at the expected location, along with the hostages. They are all currently inside the house. The two hostages are still wearing blindfolds, and their hands are still bound behind their backs. That should help identify them."

John looked around the van. All of the team members were dressed in civilian clothes. Everyone had M4 standard military-issue assault rifles. Some also carried nine-millimeter Berretta pistols.

John had left it up to each individual as to whether or not they wanted to carry a pistol. Some people felt very uncomfortable carrying only one weapon, but John had the utmost faith in the M4. To him it was like the old saying, "never bring a knife to a gunfight." Or in this case: "never bring a pistol to a rifle fight."

On the way to the rescue, Wally was driving and Sheb was in the passenger seat. Both men had dark hair and dark complexions, so at first glance it would appear that two Iraqis were just out for an early drive. The rest of the team was seated in the back and couldn't be seen because of the curtains on the windows. John was confident that they would appear just like any of the thousands of vans that drove around Baghdad every day.

The drive took only ten minutes and was uneventful; there had been some traffic in the streets, but not enough to cause concern or to interfere with the operation.

"The target is right around the corner!" Eddie announced excitedly.

As they eased the van around the corner, they saw that the hostages were being led to a car, and they were getting ready to leave. All four kidnappers were armed with AK-47s. Luckily for the team, the hostages diverted their captors' attention away from the approaching van.

"Stop the van!" John yelled.

Wally slammed on the brakes and they piled out. They were only twenty-five meters from the kidnappers so they all started firing and moving forward.

As it dawned on the kidnappers that Americans were attacking them, three of them raised their weapons to return fire while the fourth turned and ran into the house.

The three kidnappers that had decided to fight were killed in short order. Wally and Sheb secured the hostages. John motioned for Eddie and Bruce to follow him to the building to root out the fourth kidnapper. As they crept up on the building, the fourth kidnapper stepped out, his hands in the air.

The team didn't hesitate; they all shot one round at the same time. The three rounds were fired so close together that it sounded like only one shot. The kidnapper was dead before he hit the ground.

When they reached the door where the kidnapper lay, John said, "Eddie, you and Bruce check out the building. Quick search! We leave in two minutes."

John dropped another death card like the one he left for the mortar crew. Then he walked over to the other three dead kidnappers and picked up their weapons. Sheb and Wally had already loaded the hostages into the van and were waiting.

Eddie walked out of the building carrying an AK-47. He approached John and reported, "This is all we found."

John stood staring at the building and seemed to be deep in thought. Eddie asked him, "What is it, boss?"

"I hate to leave that building standing. It will probably be used again by some terrorist. From this point on we will always carry a satchel charge in every vehicle. Pre-wired, multi-purpose explosives tend to come in handy in situations like these."

They both got into the vehicle and John noticed several of the neighbors were poking their heads out their front doors or their windows. He couldn't blame them; gunfire had just erupted in their neighborhood. One Iraqi was standing outside his door and looking right at John. He raised his hand in a wave and yelled, "*Shukraan.*" John returned his wave but didn't say anything to return the thank-you. He thought it was nice that some Iraqis openly showed their gratitude for what the Americans did for them, but John could care less. If everyone in this neighborhood had known that the four kidnappers were bad people, why the hell didn't they do something about it? The fear factor was a big part, but still, there comes a time when every man should stand up for their freedom and not be controlled by fear. John thought, I guess that's why we're here!

They headed toward the Green Zone. Sheb kept the vehicle at a moderate pace, which was a good thing. Drive the same pace as everyone else on the road and you won't be noticed.

The team was elated; their adrenalin levels were at an all-time high. John talked with the Egyptian, telling him that they were transporting them to the Green Zone hospital for medical checks. The Egyptian kept asking who they were, again and again. John just replied, "We're just regular American soldiers."

8

After they dropped the hostages off at the hospital, John told Wally to pull over to the side of the road.

"Guys, I know you feel real good about yourselves, but remember the deal. If anybody asks, we have no idea who rescued the hostages. Once again, I'm not going to ask you to lie. If anyone asks me about it, I'll tell them that I don't know. But I'll let each of you decide how you want to answer."

Sheb turned around in the front seat and looked at John. "We're with you, boss."

"Okay, let's go back to the team house. I need a cup of coffee," John said, leaning back in his seat with a big smile.

Part IV
Death Comes to the Team

People who wait for all conditions to be perfect before acting, never act.

—*Unknown*

1

John and Eddie were jogging around the compound again, swapping stories about their girls.

"The way you're talking about Shelly, it sounds like you're falling for her," John stated.

"Nah. But I will admit that I like her more after one night than some other girls I've dated for months," Eddie confessed.

"You know why that is?"

"Yeah, it's because of the environment were in," Eddie said between gasps of breath. John was setting a brutal pace this morning, and Eddie was struggling to keep in stride with him. But he'd be damned if he was going to let his team sergeant pull away from him.

It had been two days since the hostages were rescued, and so far there had been no blowback. Some general inquiries had been made, so word had gotten out that there had been a rescue, but nobody could find out who had done it. John was starting to think that maybe this secret would stay a secret.

"What's on the plate for today?" Eddie asked as they rounded a corner.

"I think we need to go to FOB Falcon again. Wally said his source knows of an IED maker. Maybe Wally can get the location of the building where they're making these damn things."

They ran for another thirty minutes, never once slowing their running pace until they stated walking to cool down.

John was thinking that Eddie was getting faster; it was getting harder and harder to run with him. One of these days Eddie was going to pull away from him and leave him in the dust.

Eddie was thinking that John was getting faster; he thought he would never be able to beat him. It was getting harder and harder to maintain pace with him.

John said, "Where's Sheb this morning?"

"His knee has been bothering him again, so he decided to lift weights this morning. He should be in the weight room."

"Let's go join him. I need to work on some upper body myself."

113

They met Sheb in the weight room as expected, and for the next hour the three of them lifted weights and joked around.

Wally came in at about 0900 hours and joined them lifting weights. "I have my meeting at 1400 hours down at Falcon," he said.

"Let's leave here at 1300," John said through gritted teeth as he struggled with a 175-pound bench-press. When John lifted weights, he concentrated on doing more repetitions rather than heavy weight. His philosophy was, the more weight you put on your body, the slower it made you. It was good to be strong, but not at the expense of losing your speed and agility.

Eddie, on the other hand, was a freak. When he bench-pressed, he would go up in weight to 350 pounds. As big as Eddie was, his weight and size were never a disadvantage. He said it was all in the workout program. If you were really strong but a slow runner, you should be running more. Simple!

Sheb was sitting on the floor stretching and rubbing his injury. He cursed under his breath, "Fucking knee."

Sheb had twisted his knee on a parachute jump about a year ago. He had landed on the edge of a ditch, and his foot had stuck in the side of the ditch while the rest of his body continued to fall into the deeper portion, leaving him inverted. He had managed to walk off the drop zone, but his knee had never been the same since. The doctors said he should have it operated on, but Sheb blew it off. If he had gotten the operation he would have missed this deployment, and there was no way in hell that was going to happen.

John looked at him and nodded to indicate his knee.

"It's fine," was all Sheb said, but judging from John's expression he knew what was coming.

"Maybe you ought to hang here for a couple of days and wait for the swelling to go down. Stay here with Larry so he can monitor your knee," John said.

Sheb nodded as he stood up and said, "Okay."

John knew Sheb was pissed off about this, but one of the best things about Sheb was that he would always do whatever was best for the team, no matter what.

2

The team sat down and had lunch, which was prepared by an old Iraqi woman they had hired to cook and clean for them. Today she had prepared a large tray of goat meat over rice, with fresh salad on the side.

They discussed the day's activities. The captain told John that he was going to go along this time. Miguel and Mike both looked at John with longing in their eyes.

"Larry and Sheb will remain here; the rest of us will take two vehicles and go down to Falcon for Wally's meeting. If we have to stay there again like the other night, four guys will return here to help Sheb with his meeting tomorrow morning, while three of us will remain at Falcon if there's a need."

Sheb nodded his agreement.

Eddie looked over at John and smiled, and judging by his expression, Eddie knew that at least John and he would be staying at Falcon. There was a definite need, and that need went by the names Tanya and Shelly.

John looked around the table to see if anyone disagreed with him. Nobody raised any objections.

Miguel said, "Do you want me to bring any special weapons?"

John answered without looking up from his plate, "Bring the M79. Also, Eddie, make sure that each vehicle has a satchel charge in it."

"Already done that this morning before our run," Eddie replied.

"Good," John said. "We leave in thirty minutes."

3

Wally's meeting lasted over an hour. He was really thankful that Eddie sat in with him. Eddie was experienced with dealing with Iraqis, and he had added a lot to the interview. The key to it, Wally learned from Eddie, was asking the right questions and being patient. These were especially important when using an interpreter as they were doing now.

Wally was sure that they had gotten what they needed to target the IED maker. He was about to say they were finished, when Eddie asked a question that he would not have thought of: "Will you show us where this guy is, and where the factory is?"

Wally expected his source to decline; he had learned during this deployment that many Iraqis wanted to give out information, but few were willing to risk their own lives. He told his source to remain where he was; he would be back in thirty minutes to pick him and the interpreter up.

Eddie and Wally walked over to their small base of operations building and found everyone watching a movie. Bruce paused the movie and Wally briefed everyone on the current situation.

John was the first to speak up. "It's a rare thing to have a source willing to go along. I expect he is either being completely honest with you, or they're setting us up for an ambush. But it definitely bears a recon."

The captain added, "We need to at least go take a look. We have civilian vehicles, so the possibility of us being compromised will be negligible."

John got to thinking about the vehicle breakdown. They had the van and the Toyota truck. The van was not a problem, but the Toyota truck windows made it difficult to disguise the fact that those in it were American. Plus, the vehicle itself was a little suspicious. There weren't too many Toyota Tacomas driving around Baghdad.

"Sir, I think we should just take the van. Four of us guys, the interpreter, and the source. The rest hang back here and be ready to roll out in the Toyota just in case."

"Who do want to go?" The captain asked.

"Wally and Eddie, for sure. They are the ones working the source. As for the other two, I think it's time to let Wally make some decisions. It's his information and he can pick who he wants to go," John said.

Wally looked at John and said, "You and Miguel."

Bruce was about to say something; Wally and he were supposed to be friends. But Wally added, "I think Bruce should stay here and monitor the radio. He's the only commo guy we have, with Sheb still at the team house."

John could tell that Bruce was hurt, so he added, "That's smart planning. Let's go pick up your source and an interpreter, and go check this out. Sir, I expect we'll be back in an hour."

The captain replied with, "Okay. Be careful."

John chuckled to himself. He hated when people said that, especially in their current situation. They were ass-deep in the middle of a war and about to go check out a guy who makes bombs to kill Americans with, and someone says to be careful. Whenever someone said that John always wanted to reply with, "Nah, I'm not going to be careful." He had always held his tongue, knowing damn well that most people just said that as a reaction response. It was the same thing as the greeting, "How's it going?" Nobody really cared how it was going; they just said it to be nice.

The four Americans, a very scared interpreter, and the Iraqi source rolled out the gate and headed toward the Abu Dasheer district. John remembered this place as a congested pit of criminals. As they drove down the main street through the district, John was amazed that the place had changed so dramatically. The streets were cleaned up—not clean, but by Iraqi standards they looked pretty good. He even noticed that some of the buildings had been painted. This change was definitely a credit to the brigade stationed at Falcon, and especially to their commander.

That brigade commander was one of the smartest commanders John had ever met. John had met him several times, and he was the first full bird colonel John had ever met that liked to listen more than he liked to talk. The colonel had a grasp on the situation in south Baghdad, and the difference was evident everywhere you drove. One of the Colonel's ideas was to create jobs. Instead of buying a street sweeper for the neighborhood clean-up project, he bought five hundred brooms. Give a person a job so he can support his family and he's less likely to accept money from the terrorist organization.

When John first heard of this idea he thought it was brilliant. Looking around this neighborhood, it was apparent that the idea was also working.

They got to the end of the street and made a right turn. They saw a platoon of American soldiers, apparently guarding a construction project. John remembered now that a new school was being built. John thought, that's something that will never make it into the American media!

A sign was posted in front of the work site showing an American and an Iraqi shaking hands. There was also a logo that read, "Working hand-in-hand to create a bright future for Iraq." Another one of the colonel's brilliant ideas!

John's thoughts were interrupted by Wally's source as he pointed down a side street and started speaking rapidly. He was speaking too fast for anyone on the team to follow, so Wally looked expectantly at the interpreter.

The interpreter translated, "He says, that one story building with the red gate is the IED factory."

"Let's stop and take some pictures, and get the grid location," John said, pulling out his own camera.

The team stopped only fifty meters from the gate entrance into the bomb factory. They were parked along with other vehicles and facing the opposite direction, so nobody was worried about looking suspicious.

The red gate suddenly opened and three individuals came walking out, two of which carrying AK-47s.

The source said that the unarmed guy was the bomb manufacturer, and the two armed individuals were his bodyguards. They started to get back into the car and John said, "Wally, drive up beside that car and stop for a split second. Then when I yell 'punch it,' haul ass down the alley."

Wally glanced over his shoulder with a questioning look, but before he could say anything, John yelled at him, "I don't have time to explain it to you, now drive!"

Wally turned around and started to head for the car John had indicated. John told him to keep a normal speed. They timed it perfectly; the van pulled up beside the car undetected because the bomb maker and his guards had just seated themselves in the car, facing the other way.

John slid open the sliding door of the van, tossed the satchel charge through the open window of the car, and yelled, "Punch it!"

Seeing what John had just done, Wally didn't hesitate this time. He slammed the pedal to the floor and the van spun its tires as it screamed down the alley. Before the van could get more than fifty meters from the car, the car exploded with a definite thud that everyone in the van felt.

Wally said with excitement, "Do we need to stop and go back?"

John said, "No. Remember that army platoon that was guarding that construction site? I imagine they are sending a squad or more to investigate the source of the explosion. They'll no doubt discover the IED factory and bring in ordnance guys to clear it. So our job is done; good job on the intelligence, Wally, and I'm sorry I yelled at you."

Everyone in the van was silent for quite some time. It had happened so fast that John knew they were trying to come to grips with what had just happened.

Eddie was the first to finally speak, but it wasn't until they where entering the gate back into Falcon. "What's on the plate for the rest of the day?"

John had been thinking the same thing. "Let me brief the captain on what happened, and we'll take it from there."

Miguel finally spoke after being quiet throughout the whole operation. "He's going to be pissed."

"I don't think so. We did a recon and were presented with a target of opportunity," John said with confidence. But inside, he understood that the hard part wasn't telling the captain, but convincing him not to tell Command. Or maybe the captain could find some way of reporting it to Command in such a way that they could give credit for the hit to the regular army. The captain was a smart guy, and was a lot better with words than John was.

4

The team pulled up to their building after dropping off the source and the interpreter.

The captain could tell that something happened just by the expressions on the guys' faces as they got out of the van. He spread his hands out in a gesture that asked, "Well?"

John said, "Let's go inside and have an AAR."

After everyone was seated, John explained the sequence of events from the time they left the gate until they returned. Even after Wally and Eddie added details they thought were important, the briefing took only five minutes. It was cut-and-dried, so nobody had any questions.

The captain asked everyone to leave so he could talk to John alone. Eddie was concerned; if John got fired, he would be next in line for the team sergeant job, and he was not even close to being ready for that responsibility. Not by a long shot.

As they lingered at the vehicles, Eddie was bombarded with questions. He told everyone that he had no idea what the outcome of this situation would be, then went and sat alone with Wally. Wally asked him, "What do you think will happen?"

"My guess—and remember, this is only a guess—is that the captain is telling John he needs to stand down a little, not to take so many chances. And also that he must be able to work with Command."

"Do you think John is taking too many chances, or putting us in danger?" Wally asked softly, because he didn't want anyone else to overhear.

Eddie thought for a while before answering, "No, we are Green Berets. We are trained and paid extra money to take calculated risks. Some may think we're taking an unnecessary risk; but that's for each individual to determine, including you. But I want to make something clear. If you think you're being put into compromising situations, you need to speak up now."

Wally didn't hesitate. "I think we are doing what we have all been trained to do, what we're supposed to do, and to tell you the truth, I'm having a good time.

I don't know if that sounds right, but it's the truth; I'm having the time of my life."

Eddie slapped him on the back. "Nothing wrong with the way you feel. This is pretty goddamn fun, isn't it?"

They were both still laughing when John opened the door and told the rest of the team to come back inside.

When the team had gathered back together the captain said, "What happened today was a target of opportunity and you guys did the right thing. Unfortunately, Command will not see it that way. So this incident never happened, and since it never happened there's no reason to report it. Does everyone understand this?" The captain waited until he got nods from all the team members before he continued. "Right now myself, Bruce, Mike, and Miguel will head back to the team house. In the morning we will go with Sheb to his meeting."

"John, Eddie, and Wally will remain here to do a follow-up on the explosion. Find out if the army guys found the IED factory, or if there's any more information to be had from Wally's source."

When the captain had finished, Eddie asked, "How long do we have to stay down here?"

"Shouldn't be more than a couple of days, but I'll let John determine that. The main thing is for you guys to get as much intelligence about this IED factory as you can. Where's the stuff coming from? How are they hauling it? How sophisticated is the technology? Are they still using command-detonated IEDs, or have they switched to remote-detonation triggering devices? These are the questions we need to try and answer, so there are many things to follow up on. It should keep you busy for a couple of days."

After waiting to see if there were any more questions, the captain rose to leave. He added, "If we need you guys to help us tomorrow, I'll call you. I will call down to inform you of the outcome of Sheb's meeting as well." With that the captain strode out of the room.

5

They had barely turned the corner to leave when Eddie looked at John and said, "You going to tell us what happened?"

John smiled. "Of course, but let's go inside and crack a beer. I can talk better with a little booze in me."

It never ceased to amaze Eddie how nothing seemed to bother John, at least nothing showed on the surface. He began to think John was as cold-blooded as people had said.

John popped a beer and laid out his story for them. "The captain was not mad, although he did feel that I was a little too cavalier with my tactical decisions and after listening to him talk, he made a good point. I was somewhat surprised when he decided not to report this incident, but I can bet we will never get away with this type of operation again."

He paused for a moment, then carried on. "Look, the bottom line, is our job is to conduct unconventional warfare, and that's what we did. We are the only ones in this area who have the freedom to move about in the populace and do these types of unconventional hits. The war is already a year old, and the terrorists have changed their tactics several times. Yet, we are doing the same types of hits on targets we did on day one. The terrorists are not stupid; they know what our tactics are, if we don't change them up all the time we're going to get our asses kicked."

Eddie and Wally both nodded their heads in agreement, and then Eddie said, "Did he bring up the ATM incident in Nashville?"

John nodded. "After the captain brought that up, I could see his point about taking risks."

Wally was in the dark, so he asked, "What's the ATM incident?"

John and Eddie looked at each other and started laughing. Eddie said, "Do you want me to tell it?"

"Nah let me tell it. You always screw it up." John sat back and thought where to begin …

6

Nashville, Tennessee 2002

Nashville had recently had a series of holdups at ATMs. By the time John first read about it in the paper, there had already been four robberies within as many weeks.

The robberies all had the same characteristics. They always occurred between midnight and four in the morning, and always on a weekday. Two of the robberies had happened on Mondays, one on a Tuesday, and the last one on a Wednesday.

From eyewitness accounts, it had been concluded that there were two robbers. Both were described as lean and athletic looking men. Their heights were given as five feet, five inches and five feet, seven inches. There was no description of the faces because both men had worn plain, black ski masks. The rest of their clothing was also non-descriptive.

The witnesses all agreed that they believed the criminals to be white males, this being determined by their speech patterns.

The suspects hadn't used guns during the holdups; from the description given by the victims, both robbers had brandished kitchen knives. They had proved their willingness to use the knives at the second holdup when a man had tried to resist and sustained a nasty slash in his leg for his heroism and still lost all his money.

No video surveillance was available because the robbers had waited for their victims to leave the camera's field of view.

The police had stepped up their patrols since the first robbery, but the extra patrols had had no effect, as indicated by the fact that three more robberies had occurred.

The criminals were described as very patient and methodical; they had selected their victims carefully, waiting for the weakest before striking. The first two victims had been elderly men, one of which suffered the cut in the leg. The third victim had been a young college girl from Minnesota who'd been out parting all night with her friends, and needed some cash. The last victim had been an obese, middle-aged woman who had been drunk when she was robbed. All the victims had been alone.

The robbery locations had seemed random; the only thing distinct about them was that all of the robberies had been carried out on the east side of Interstate 24 and north of Interstate 40.

So with all this information, John came up with a plan. It was obvious to him that the seeming-randomness of the attacks was actually the very pattern the police should be looking at.

John had found out all this information on a Thursday and he immediately went into action. He disguised himself as an older man and drove the two hours to Nashville that same afternoon. He spent the afternoon scouting ATMs that were in the most remote locations, and he picked out four at which he would try his plan. He sat back and waited for midnight.

When midnight rolled around, John splashed some whiskey on his face and staggered up to the first ATM, walking like he was drunk. He dropped his wallet as he approached the machine, as part of the act. Taking his time, he drew out one hundred dollars then staggered back to his car. Nothing happened.

He drove to the second ATM, and parked well back from the surveillance cameras. He went through the same routine and again, but once more, nothing happened.

It was close to two in the morning when he arrived at the third ATM. He parked his car, once again out of the range of the surveillance cameras. He staggered across the parking lot, reached into his back pocket for his wallet, and dropped it. He stood swaying on his feet as he waited for the machine to spit out his money. Finally, with the money in hand, he started to stagger back to his car. He didn't put the money in his wallet right away; he counted it several times as he crossed the parking lot. As he approached the car he put his wallet away, and there they were!

The robbers approached John fast, both with their knives out in front of them.

"Give us your money, now!" The shorter one yelled.

John hit him!

The robber's head snapped back like it had been broken open and he dropped in a heap at John's feet. John had to hand it to the other robber; he didn't back away or even appear to be scared, but slashed at John with his knife. It was a wide arm slash, and John easily parried it aside.

Realization had now set in the robber's eyes. The stooped over, drunken old man that they had observed taking money from the ATM no longer existed.

Instead, a tall man with wide shoulders and an evil glint in his eyes now faced him. The man's eyes appeared silver and shined like cat's eyes at night, but the most unsettling thing was that the man was smiling.

The robber stabbed in straight with the knife, but the man slapped it away so casually that he almost seemed bored. And then he spoke.

"Young man, if you're prepared to kill me then you must be prepared to die. I would happily oblige you, but judging by your eyes I can tell you're not ready to die. Think about this—if you kill me you will go to jail for the rest of your life, but I could easily kill you in self-defense and be labeled as a hero."

John waited for this to sink in. He saw the knife-wielder looking around nervously, and knew what he was thinking. John spoke again, "Don't even think about running, young man, because I can catch you before you get out of the parking lot. If you run, I will catch you. And when I catch you, I will kill you!"

Something in the tone of the tall man's voice made the robber realize he was telling the truth. The robber also knew he didn't stand a chance against this man, so he dropped the knife.

When the man spoke again, the robber thought he almost sounded disappointed that it was over and there wasn't going to be a fight. He said, "Just sit down next to your friend while I call the police."

7

John took a swallow of beer and looked at Wally. "That's it."

Wally said, "Wait a minute. I have a ton of questions."

Eddie stopped him before he could ask them. "Let me finish the story."

"When the cops arrived, John had a lot to answer for—the disguise, why he smelled of booze but wasn't drunk. Anyway, he spent the next day explaining all the events, over and over. He told the cops that it was plain to him that the robbers were teenage boys because of their size. They were not professional; the money they tried to steal was in too-small amounts. So John figured it was either drug addicts, or teenage boys, or a combination of the two. They were both small men and at first John suspected a couple of Hispanic men. But eyewitnesses said they could tell they where white men by their voices. That left only punk kids or two really small guys as possibilities. Since they were both lean in the body, the drug thing came into play. John was right; they turned out to be two sixteen-year-old punk kids with a little crack problem."

Eddie grabbed another beer before continuing. "John figured out which night they would attack again by realizing that the kids were going out of their way to make the attacks look random. The first two robberies were on Mondays, but the kids came to the conclusion that they couldn't keep attacking on the same night, for the fear of setting a pattern and getting caught. So the following week they planned their next attack for a Tuesday. The last attack came on a Wednesday. So by trying to keep it random they had inadvertently followed the days of the week. The next logical night was Thursday."

"The location was the next thing; by looking at the map it was clear that they were working the same general area, although that area was big. There were only so many ATMs that suited their style. If they were teenagers with a drug problem, they probably wouldn't have a car, so the ATMs would also have to have been in walking distance."

Eddie paused because when he had first heard the story, he hadn't believed it until someone showed him a newspaper clipping with the details. The article read:

GREEN BERET FOILS ATM ROBBERY

The rash of ATM robberies that have plagued the Nashville area the last month came to an abrupt and dramatic end Thursday night thanks to a Fort Campbell soldier.

A spokesman for the Nashville police said the two robbers, both of whom were sixteen years old, picked the wrong victim …

Wally sat in silence trying to grasp what he had just heard. Finally he looked at John and asked, "Why did you do it?"

John shrugged his shoulders. "Thought it might be fun."

"What did the cops say about all this?"

"They told me to go home, and to leave the police work to them in the future," John answered.

Wally certainly found a new admiration for his team sergeant. They had told him when he had come to the team that John Smith was a little crazy, and now he believed it.

"Now, since that is out of the way, I say we go talk to the unit that investigated the explosion and cleaned out the IED factory. Let's go see what we can find out," Eddie recommended.

John said, "Let's you and I do that. Wally, call your source and ask him to come in tomorrow morning. We'll meet you at the dining facility tonight at 1800 to discuss where we're at."

John and Eddie downed their beers then locked all their gear in the operations room. The team split off in two directions; Wally broke off to find an interpreter to help with the phone call to his source, while John and Eddie went to the unit headquarters to find any information they could about the explosion, and if there had been a search of the IED factory.

8

The teammates finally all met at the dining facility at 1815 hours that evening. They ate and discussed the information they had gathered. The Explosive Ordnance Disposal unit had secured all the IED materials into a safe location, and Eddie was planning to go there in the morning to look at the explosives. It had taken a large truck to load all the materials from the factory. The IEDs had mostly been made from 155-millimeter artillery rounds with a fuse cap inserted into the cone. It turned out the terrorists were still detonating the bombs by wire connection.

Even though EOD told Eddie that they had found no remote equipment, Eddie wanted to see for himself. Just like other tactics the terrorists used—and constantly changed—Eddie was confident that the bad guys would soon vary their forms of detonation devices for IEDs.

Wally talked about the conversation he had with his source. Apparently, the source lived across the street from the factory, and had observed many vehicles coming and going over the past few weeks. Wally was confident that he would be able to get some descriptions in the morning, not only of the vehicles but of the people driving them as well.

John was satisfied they had done all they could tonight, and was lost in his own thoughts when Eddie jerked his head indicating that John should look over his shoulder.

There they sat, Tanya and Shelly.

Wally looked at them and then back at his food. "Just great. You guys get pussy, but I'm the one getting fucked."

John said, "The night is young, plenty of women running around."

Before Wally could reply, the girls sat down and joined them.

Tanya spoke first. "What's the plan?"

John looked at her and smiled, "After dinner I'm going to grab a shower, go over to our building, and watch a movie. Have a few beers, then pop a Viagra. You interested in an all-nighter?"

"Take your best shot, Green Beret," Tanya said without hesitating.

Wally shook his head, wondering how in the hell that shit worked on a woman. He couldn't even say stuff like that to his wife without getting slapped. He made a mental note to ask John what his secret was. He looked at Eddie and realized he had scored for later, also. Wally scanned the dining room. He spotted about ten different women, but none that he would cheat on his wife with. He had felt a little guilty after their party with the Iraqi women and chastised himself for being so shallow. He finally decided that he would spend the night alone.

The girls said they would be over to the building at 2030.

As Eddie, John, and Wally walked back to their building to get their shower equipment, Wally had to ask, "How do you do it? You told her what you wanted and she jumped at the chance to please you, and she's half your age!"

John walked on for another ten paces before he answered. Even Eddie wanted to hear this; he had watched John for the last year pick up women with no effort at all. Eddie even remembered one time when the team was tasked to be an Honor Guard at a funeral for a retired Green Beret that had served in Vietnam. The team was honored to do it, and the job went off without a hitch. After the funeral, they sat around and swapped stories with the Vietnam veterans at the reception. Eddie went outside for some fresh air, and while he stood against the wall of the building he noticed that the van they had driven in was rocking back and forth. He knew what was going on, but couldn't believe it until he peeked in the window. There was John, lying on his back with a cousin of the deceased, naked, riding on top of him. When he asked John about it later, his only reply was, "She asked me to fuck her because she wanted to feel good."

Now, with the way John was taking his time to answer, Eddie expected the true secret to John's success with women to come out.

John said, "I just don't care."

Wally looked at Eddie, and then back at John. "What? That's it?"

John said it was hard to explain and the conversation was dropped.

After they had all taken showers, they kicked back in the operations room, drinking beer and watching the movie *Predator*.

Wally was still agitated by John's answer, and he just had to know more. He reached over and hit pause on the computer.

"I need a better answer," Wally said to John, looking at Eddie for support.

Eddie added, "Come on, what's your secret?"

John realized they would continue to bug him until he could come up with a satisfactory answer.

"All right, there are three steps to picking up women. What I told you before was the truth. 'I don't care' was probably not the right phrase. It starts with attitude. Everything in life is second to a positive attitude. Positive attitude, confidence, passion, enthusiasm, or whatever you want to call it, is the first step at being successful at anything. I say that it's the attitude that gets things done." John paused for a minute and tried to think of another way to put it.

"Wally, you remember Selection, the first phase of becoming a Green Beret?"

"Of course I remember. You were one of the instructors."

"I want you to take your time and think real carefully. If you could only use one word to describe what got you through that course, what would it be?" John grabbed another beer while Wally spent a couple of minutes thinking about it. Eddie was smiling.

Finally, Wally said, "Guts!"

"Wouldn't you say that is just another word for positive attitude, or maybe will power?

"Okay, I see what you mean. I went to Selection with the attitude that I was going to make it, and I did!" Wally said with recognition.

"That's right. The school could have been twice as long and twice as hard, but you still would have made it because you had a positive attitude."

Eddie said, "Okay, we now know the first step in picking up women, a positive attitude. So what's the next step?"

"Understand the enemy! Women may not act like it, but they are as superficial as men. Many women say they want a man with a big heart, caring, honest, and I expect the ones who are looking for long-term relationships really do want that. But the bottom line is, when it comes to sex, women want someone who looks good."

"I remember a study I read twenty years ago. It said that most women make up their minds in the first five minutes of meeting a man whether or not she would have sex with him. That's why I work out so hard; the better I look, the better my odds," John added.

They laughed through this whole monolog, so John thought of another analogy.

"It's the same as understanding any genre you're dealing with. Let me ask you a quick question: when will the fighting here stop?"

Eddie and Wally said simultaneously, "Never." Then Wally added, "Because these people are evil."

"You are right about it never ending. Terrorism is the same as crime in the United States. It may be marginalized at times, but it will never end. But you're so wrong about why. You say terrorists are evil. Nothing could be further from the truth."

"Now hold on!" Eddie was exasperated. "Are you saying the terrorists are good people?"

"No. Wally said they were evil, but that's his point of view. Now look at it from the terrorist's point of view. They believe with all their hearts that they are doing God's work. In fact, they believe in it so much that they are willing to strap bombs to their bodies and blow people up, not really caring who they kill—men, women, children, dogs, cows, whatever. Being a martyr guarantees their entrance into heaven. I'm not saying I agree with it, I'm just saying you need to understand how they think. It's about understanding the enemy."

Eddie said, "Okay, enough analogies, we get the point. You said there were three steps in picking up a woman. Number one, positive attitude. Number two, understanding women. What's the third step?"

"The third step is the easiest: be selfless. The only thing that matters is her. Whether you're involved in conversation or sex, she should be the only thing that matters."

"That's about all there is to it. There are other small details to keep in mind, like being honest and saying the right thing at the right time, but if you can master the three steps, you shouldn't want for female company."

"I think the girls are coming," Eddie said.

Tanya and Shelly came into the room, all smiles.

Everybody knew it would be a fun night.

9

0500

Morning came too soon; John rolled over and looked at his watch.

This was the latest he had been in bed since coming to Iraq three months ago.

He looked over at Tanya and saw that she was still deep in sleep. He thought, let her sleep a while; she earned it last night.

John lay on his back staring at the ceiling. He started to reminisce about the last three months, and especially about the conversation he had with the captain yesterday.

It was clear that he had taken some chances that a lot of people would call crazy, but he still didn't see it that way. The only way to fight this war was with brutality, not diplomacy.

He thought about the fighting out in Fallujah. The brutality they had used while moving through the streets was extremely effective. He knew the consequences of detaining someone as opposed to killing them. If you detained a terrorist, you had done a couple of things in favor of the insurgency.

One: By putting a terrorist in jail you allowed him the ability to talk with other terrorists and plan possible future attacks. Plus, the terrorist organization would look after his family while he sat in jail.

Two: When the terrorist got out of jail, which he eventually would, he would be rested. He'd have learned from his mistakes, and gained a firsthand knowledge of American tactics, and he or she would kill again.

Maybe John was wrong; he didn't know for sure.

But John knew he was right about one thing, and that was the beautiful young girl sleeping beside him. It was time to wake her up; the Viagra was still working!

10

0700

Sheb had expected some good information from his source. A weapons cache, information on insurgency structure—something like that. But instead, his source told just him about a building that was used to print anti-Coalition propaganda.

The captain thought it was great information and typed up a Con-op immediately. Sheb knew it would be one of those hits where the bad guys had no weapons, and the team would have to detain someone. Then they'd spend the next two days presenting evidence and giving witness statements. The bad guys would sit a couple months in Abu Ghraib jail and then be released. Eventually the Americans would have to go after those guys again. It reminded him of a bass tournament he fished in once—catch and release.

The captain finished the Con-op and sent it to the B-team for approval. They wanted to do the hit at 0900 because his source said the enemy would be printing leaflets all morning. Sheb thought, let's hope this one gets approved!

Sheb knew they had plenty of time to get ready. He walked to the window and looked out. Miguel, Bruce, and Mike were prepping the vehicles. Everything looked ready; Larry would be staying at the team house while the other five of them did the hit.

Sheb asked the captain, without turning around, "Should we call the guys down at Falcon and bring them up for this?"

The captain said there was no need. Two vehicles with five guys were plenty to do this hit. He reemphasized that it was a low-risk target.

Sheb knew they could do the hit, but still, he always felt more comfortable with John around. The captain broke his train of thought, saying, "They approved the Con-op, but we have to take a Hummer on the hit. They don't want us going on a hit without the support of a military vehicle."

Sheb sat down and looked at the seating chart for the vehicles. "It'll be Miguel, Bruce, and myself in the Hummer. You and Mike in the Nissan truck." He looked up at the captain for confirmation.

"Sounds good. I'll call John and let him know what are plans are."

The captain dialed the phone and watched as Sheb left to tell the other guys their plan. The captain also knew that this wouldn't go over well with John; a Hummer was a big target.

11

0730

Eddie was still in bed when the phone rang. Although he wasn't sleeping, he was engaged in something very important.

He looked at Shelly and said, "Hold that thought."

Eddie listened to the captain as he explained what was about to happen. He asked if they should come to the team house. The captain told him it wasn't necessary, and asked Eddie to inform John of what was going on.

Instead of getting out of bed, Eddie yelled to the next room, "John! Can you hear me?"

The only reply was a muffled, "Yes."

"The guys at the team house are going to do a hit at 0900. They said they didn't need our help. They're taking everyone on the hit except Larry. They're going to use the Nissan truck and one of the Hummers." Eddie waited for a reply from John, but he heard only silence. A little concerned, he said, "Hey, John, did you hear me?"

Finally John replied, "Yes, I heard you. Meet me in the operations room at 0800."

"Okay," Eddie said, and then he quickly shifted his attention to Shelly. "Come on, girl, let's get to it!"

When Eddie came out of his room, Tanya was already outside waiting for Shelly. Tanya spoke to Eddie, "John is in the operations room already."

"Thanks." He gave a quick goodbye to Shelly and walked into the operations room.

Wally was sitting in a chair with a worried look on his face as John talked to the captain on the phone. Eddie listened in on John's side of the conversation.

"Is that a wise choice?"

"There's no way you can talk them out of it?"

"All right sir, let us know how you guys do."

John laid the phone down and leaned back in his chair with a frown on his face.

Eddie couldn't stand the suspense. "What was that all about?"

"They were told they had to use a Hummer on the hit."

Wally said, "Boss, this is probably a stupid question, but so what?"

John replied, "How many civilian vehicles have been hit by IEDs?"

"None that I know of."

"Now, how many Hummers have been destroyed by IEDs?"

"Bunches."

"It's probably nothing. I just know that a Hummer is a prime target." John mumbled something else that neither Wally nor Eddie could hear, but then he said, "They said everything's under control, and they'll call us when it's over to give us an update." He stood up suddenly. "Who's for breakfast?"

12

0940

Eddie checked his camera and laid out his notes. He wanted to make absolutely certain he had enough battery power to capture on film everything from every possible angle at the IED factory. If he could document and memorize all the details of the confiscated weaponry, he was sure that the next time an IED was detonated—and there would definitely be more IEDs—he would have a good chance of identifying what specific types of munitions were used, and in turn maybe tell how, where, and who had built it. Eddie realized it would take a huge database, but he had already amassed a good deal of data on IED explosions. Today was going to be exciting, he thought. He had never had the opportunity to study IED material in its raw state.

John watched him, amazed at the simplicity of Eddie's data. He used a very simple technique to organize his database, the Who, What, Where, When, Why, and How approach. Eddie noticed John intently staring at the papers that were spread out on the table. "Would you like me to explain what I'm doing?" Eddie asked.

John scooted his chair closer. "Yes, walk me through it."

Eddie began, passionately, "The first question I ask myself is "Why?" This just happens to be the easiest to answer. Why are they using IEDs? The answer is large effect with minimal risk. Simplicity in the construction. And last, but not least, the ready availability of materials. Then I look at a way to get rid of the "Why" for the terrorists. At our level, the best we can do is to make the streets miserable for the IED people, like we did yesterday."

"That makes sense," John replied.

Eddie continued. "The next two go hand in hand—the "How" and the "What." This stack of papers is everything I have collected on how the IEDs are constructed, how they are being emplaced, how they are being transported, what materials are being used, and so on. Today I hope to add several papers and photographs to this portion of the database. This material should give us some patterns, and maybe we can predict what direction the bad guys are headed with their methods. For instance, I believe there will be more remote detonation devices in the future, and the bombs will be more powerful."

"When did you start putting all this together?" John said, impressed.

"Before we ever got here, and I've been updating and adding to it ever since."

Eddie spread a Baghdad city map on the table; the map was covered with handwritten numbers in red ink. "Every one of these numbers indicates the location of an IED attack. Look at number fifteen, just south of the refinery. Let's say you wanted more information about that particular attack. Just grab this book and look up number fifteen, and it will tell you all the details of the attack, including the time."

Eddie handed the book to John, and once again John was impressed. Every number had detailed descriptions of an attack, and some included photographs of the damage to a particular vehicle, while other pictures showed things like the hole left from the detonation, including detailed measurements.

"Damn, Eddie, this is amazing!"

"Thanks. I would like you to sit down with me and see if there are any patterns emerging. Maybe you can see something I ain't catching," Eddie said expectantly.

"We'll have to set aside a couple days, there's lots of material here," John said as he continued sifting through the papers.

Eddie and John were so engrossed in studying the material that they both jumped when the phone rang. Eddie picked it up. "This is Eddie."

Eddie handed the phone straight to John. "It's the captain, and he wants to talk with you. You know, if you would turn on your own damn phone, it would make life a lot easier for me."

Eddie went back to his notes and started studying diagrams and pictures of detonating devices that he had already seen.

"Shit," John said into the phone.

Eddie looked over and saw that John was bending over at the waist, rubbing his forehead with one hand as he listened on the phone.

"Okay, sir. We're on our way." John handed the phone back to Eddie. "We need to go to the Green Zone. The Hummer was hit by an IED."

"Anyone hurt?"

"Miguel and Bruce just got some scratches, but Sheb was hurt pretty bad," John said, grabbing his gear. "Wally should be close to finishing his meeting. We'll pick him up on the way out."

13

1020

They rode in silence to the Green Zone, everyone thinking the same thing. Why in the fuck were they told to take a Hummer?

They pulled up to the hospital and could tell by the level of activity that everyone had been alerted to the incident. As they exited the van, John noticed that everyone from Company headquarters was already there, along with a lot of people milling about that he didn't recognize. He figured that the people he didn't recognize must be from the Battalion headquarters.

The captain came out the front door of the hospital to meet John halfway across the parking area. "I have bad news ... Sheb has died. He never regained consciousness after the IED exploded."

John, Eddie, and Wally froze in their tracks.

"How are Bruce and Miguel?" John managed to ask after a long silence.

"They're fine. Some scratches and cuts, maybe some eardrum damage, but they'll be able to go back to the team house today."

"Let's go inside and see them."

The captain laid out the details of what happened while they walked through the hospital, but nobody was listening.

"Hey, boss," Miguel said to John as he walked into the room. John noticed his arm was wrapped in bandages from the wrist to the elbow. "It's just a scratch; I'll be back in the game within the hour."

Bruce was standing at the door. He had a bandage on his leg and another one on his face. Before John could say anything, Bruce put a hand on his face. "Just a shaving cut."

The battalion commander said, "Would you like to see Sheb?"

Eddie and John looked at each other. Eddie was about to say something when John shook his head and put his finger to his lips, indicating to him to be quiet. He motioned for them to go outside.

The sergeant major caught John in the hallway. "I want to say I'm sorry; I know you and Sheb were close."

John just nodded and continued to walk outside.

John and Eddie sat on the curb in front of the hospital. Both of them had known Sheb for a few years. They sat in silence, each with their own thoughts.

"John?" Eddie said without looking at him.

"Yeah." John also continued to look straight ahead.

"Thanks for pulling me out of there. I'm afraid I would have said something bad to the commander."

John didn't reply. He couldn't blame Eddie for being mad or wanting to blame someone for Sheb's death. They had already voiced their opinion on the fact that driving around in military vehicles was more dangerous than conducting operations in civilian vehicles. It was obvious to everyone that the decision to use a Hummer on the hit had caused Sheb's death, and there was no point in stating that to any commander and possibly getting yourself in trouble for insubordination.

They both sat in silence. Eventually, Wally joined them on the curb. He said, "I liked him."

John looked at Wally and patted him on the back. "Everyone liked Sheb."

"Now what?" Wally asked.

Eddie answered, "We have three months over here yet, so we pick ourselves up and go back to work."

"That's right," John agreed.

"Just like that?"

"Just like that. Don't forget we'll be back here next year." John wanted to say more to reassure Wally, but instead he remained silent.

Wally stared straight ahead. "It never ends, does it?"

John and Eddie answered together. "No."

Epilogue

Shebley Martin Henderson was buried with full military honors in his hometown of Dallas, Texas. He was awarded the Bronze Star medal with V (for "valor") device and the Purple Heart, posthumously. His wife and two children moved back to Texas and have moved on with their lives.

Nobody from the team was able to attend Sheb's funeral because of the remaining commitment they had in Iraq, but on returning to the United States in July of 2004, John and Eddie drove to Dallas and visited his grave. To pay their respects, they went to a local bar, picked up two women, and partied for three straight days. They felt that Sheb would have liked that.

ODA 451 continued to fight the insurgency for three more months, fighting gallantly. They didn't achieve the same level of success that they had in the first three months of the deployment, according to official reports. Unofficial and unreported, they continued to terrorize the insurgents to the point that a bounty was put on the heads of John Smith and Eddie Hardy, but that's another story!

The town of Fallujah was eventually cleared, however the second assault had cost many more lives because the terrorists had used the "negotiating time" to fortify their defensive positions.

After the team conducted the ambush on the mortar crew that had been terrorizing them, they were never mortared again. It seemed that the "death card" that appeared on several more dead terrorists and its psychological impact was enough to quell the attacks in the Al Rasheed district. Such attacks went from an average of thirty per month to only two or three per month.

The operation in which the Indian and Egyptian truck drivers were rescued remains a secret. To this day, nobody knows who conducted the rescue, including the two truck drivers. The only information about the operation that came to light was the Egyptian's statement. He said that he was sure they were United States soldiers, and one of them had weird, silver-looking eyes.

The satchel charge that John Smith threw into the window of the IED manufacturer's car killed all three terrorists and started the car on fire. All three were burnt to a crisp.

John Smith continued to have the occasional rendezvous with Tanya, the beautiful young girl he had met at the smoothie bar, for the remaining three months he spent in Iraq. However, after deploying back to the United States he never heard from her again.

Thankfully, John never needed to use the picture of Jeff and the Iraqi girl that he had taken, but he still had it saved electronically, just in case.

John Smith remained as the team sergeant of ODA 451.

Eddie Hardy still met with Shelly whenever the opportunity arose, but they, too, drifted apart and never saw one another again. Eddie was made the intelligence sergeant when the team returned to the States.

Wally Granner went back to his wife with a newfound respect for her. He vowed never to cheat on her again, and to honor his commitment and the word that he had given her. Wally replaced Eddie as the senior engineer sergeant.

Larry Masson attended combat stress counseling. It was determined that he was combat-ineffective, and he was diagnosed with posttraumatic stress disorder. He was discharged from the army with full disability, and was never heard from again. A rumor did circulate that he had joined the ACLU and had become an anti-war activist, but this rumor was never substantiated.

Bruce Stern got a divorce from his wife within six months of his return from Iraq. She had had another man living with her during the entire time Bruce was deployed. Bruce didn't complain or get mad at the situation; he had cheated on his wife while in Iraq, and so he admitted that he had gotten what he deserved. Bruce unenthusiastically replaced Sheb as the senior communications sergeant.

Miguel Sanchez became the senior weapons sergeant after Jeff Wallace was fired.

Jeff Wallace left the army. He had convinced himself that nobody was as smart as he was. He also believed that everyone was out to get him, and he would never receive a fair shake. He now works as his own boss as a drywall contractor.

Mike Vomage also left the service to pursue a civilian career in medicine.

Captain Rinehart left the team because his time as a detachment commander was up. He was assigned a staff position at the Battalion level.

John Smith's twenty rules and observations

Special Forces—Talks about how he is and thinks he is the best soldier.
Green Beret—Proves he is the best by his actions.

Special Forces—Talks about how to solve a problem.
Green Beret—Just fixes it.

Special Forces—Complains about a problem.
Green Beret—Finds a solution and solves the problem.

Special Forces—Tells stories about what he used to do.
Green Beret—Only cares about what he's doing and what he's going to do.

Special Forces—Trains in hand-to-hand combat with an instructor.
Green Beret—Goes to a bar and picks a fight with the biggest guy.

Special Forces—Detains a bad guy in an attempt to gain intelligence.
Green Beret—Kills the bad guy.

Special Forces—Tries to do the right thing.
Green Beret—Does whatever it takes to get the job done.

Special Forces—Expects accolades for his actions.
Green Beret—Remains the quiet professional.

Special Forces—Survives on the battlefield by conducting "what if" planning.
Green Beret—Survives on the battlefield by conducting "what is" planning.

Special Forces—Loves to give his opinion.
Green Beret—Will give his opinion if asked.

Special Forces—When something is broken his first thought is, "Who can I call to get this fixed?"
Green Beret—When something is broken his first thought is, "How can I fix this?"

Special Forces—When the bullets start flying the first action he takes is to call Command.
Green Beret—When the bullets start flying the first action he takes is to shoot.

Special Forces—Makes it a point to state the obvious.
Green Beret—Ignores the obvious.

Special Forces—Looks over your shoulder when you're working on a computer to see what you're doing.
Green Beret—Doesn't care, unless it pertains to him

Special Forces—Will cock-block every chance he can.
Green Beret—Will help you get laid.

Special Forces—Goes to his team sergeant with a problem.
Green Beret—Goes to his team sergeant with a problem and a solution.

Special Forces—Is a pessimist.
Green Beret—Is an optimist.

Special Forces—Blames his mistakes on someone else.
Green Beret—Admits when he is wrong.

Special Forces—Cheats on his wife while on deployment.
Green Beret—Doesn't cheat on his wife, ever.

Special Forces—Will be sympathetic when you have a personal problem.
Green Beret—Calls you a pussy.

About the Author

Jay Mann is a retired U.S. Army Master Sergeant. He served for fifteen years as a Green Beret and five years in military intelligence. He served one combat tour each in Somalia and Afghanistan, and two in Iraq. He now lives a quiet life by himself in the hills of western Tennessee.

978-0-595-68994-1
0-595-68994-9

CPSIA information can be obtained
at www.ICGtesting.com
Printed in the USA
BVHW040741200822
645068BV00009BA/55/J